# A Martian Poet in Siberia

## By

## Duncan Hunter

This book is a work of fiction. Places, events, and situations
in this story are purely fictional. Any resemblance to actual
persons, living or dead, is coincidental.

ISBN: 1-4033-2356-9 (e-book)
ISBN: 1-4033-2357-7 (Paperback)

This book is printed on acid free paper.

1stBooks - rev. 12/13/02

**For
Chu Ti
Alex and Claire**

# Acknowledgements

p. 4: from Lance, in *Nabokov's Dozen*, London: Penguin Books, 1960. (rights: Weidenfeld & Nicholson).

p. 29: from Sad Steps, in *High Windows*, Philip Larkin, London: Faber and Faber, 1974.

P. 53: Excerpt from Earl of Rochester's translation (circa 1674) of Seneca's *Trojan Women*, cited in *The Size of Thoughts*, Nicholson Baker, London: Vintage, 1997.

p. 63-64: Early Morning from *The Selected Poems of Janet Lewis* (Ohio University Press/Swallow Press, 2000). Reprinted with the permission of Ohio University Press, Athens, Ohio.

p. 64, 171-172: From *Poems Old and New, 1918-1978* by Janet Lewis (Ohio University Press/Swallow Press, 1982). Reprinted with the permission of Ohio University Press, Athens, Ohio.

p. 65-66: From *The Fig Tree – Memoirs of a Taiwanese Patriot* by Wu Zhuoliu, (Duncan Hunter, trans.), 1stBooks Library. Copyright © 2002. Reprinted by permission of the translator.

p. 100: From Vulture (rights: Random House, Inc.), from *The Selected Poetry of Robinson Jeffers*, edited by Tim Hunt, Stanford University Press, 2001.

p. 111: From "You, Andrew Marvell", from *Collected Poems, 1917-1982* by Archibald MacLeish. Copyright © 1985 by The Estate of Archibald MacLeish. Reprinted by permission of Houghton Mifflin Company. All rights reserved.

# Selected References

Carson, R., *The Sea around Us,* New York: Oxford University Press, 1979.

Dyson, F., *Infinite in all directions,* London: Penguin Books, 1989.

Ehrlich, P.R., Carl Sagan, et al., *The Cold and the Dark – The World after Nuclear War,* New York: W.W. Norton & Company, 1984.

Hoppal, Mihaly, *Nature Worship in Siberian Shamanism,* at http://haldjas.folklore.ee/folklore/vol4/hoppal.html

Lebedev, V., *Diary of a Cosmonaut,* (Luba Diangar, trans.), New York: Bantam Books, 1990.

Lewis J.S., *Rain of Iron and Ice,* Reading, Massachusetts: Addison Wesley, 1996.

Lopez B.H., *Arctic Dreams: imagination and desire in a northern landscape,* New York: Scribner, 1986.

Lovelock, J., *Gaia: a new look at life on Earth,* Oxford: OUP, 1979.

Moore, P., *On Mars,* London: Cassell, 1998.

Needham J., *Science and Civilization in China, vols. II, IV,* Cambridge: Cambridge University Press, 1954.

Pearce, D., *Brave New World? A Defence of Paradise-Engineering* at http://www.huxley.net

Phillips R., *"Forest Beatniks" and "Urban Thoreaus",* New York: Peter Lang, 2000.

Schama, S., *Landscape and Memory,* New York: A.A. Knopf, 1985.

Shaw, H. R., *Craters, Cosmos and Chronicles – a new theory of Earth*, Stanford: Stanford University Press, 1994.

Singer, P., *Animal Liberation*, London: Cape, 1976.

Zubrin, R. (with Richard Wagner), *The Case for Mars*, New York: The Free Press, 1996.

# <u>Who I am</u>

My name is Han.

By ancestry I am what used to be called Eurasian. But at times like these such labels are irrelevant. Now I am a citizen of the world - at home everywhere and nowhere.

An exaggeration? An inflated sense of my own cosmopolitan credentials? Had I been of this world before what happened happened there might have been some justification for such a reproach, but I assure you I mean the words literally, flatly, with no intent to burnish my ego by uttering them, or to deflate yours, whoever you are, who finds this chronicle. In its pages is a record of our life here, of our life before, jotted down over the last eight or so years.

In fact my sense of identity is now, if anything, as much zoological (I am only half joking) as cultural or national. Empty terms now, for what else could such an event induce in one as a surviving human but a hitherto non-existent *species*-awareness, a vertiginous new take on the role and purpose of one's existence as a now rare human animal? For we (by which I mean myself, my nine fellow Settlers, the twenty-nine we have become, and the two we found here) are now humanity. The pyramid has been inverted - we are the apex above which the rest of the massive structure has yet to reappear, pregnant though we are with the seeds which might (I had written *will)* make it possible.

We, the Settlers, were the culmination of that intense surge of knowledge which began in the last century and a half of the second millennium and

1

pushed us further and faster than our frail legs could properly carry us. From Omega we have become Alpha, and the slow plod starts again. With a difference: we have been there; we have known the concupiscence of knowledge, had drunk its heady brew and arrogantly set off for the future which is now the past. We know what we are capable of. We had stood between the cusps of the routine and the impossible, and slid unthinkingly towards the latter. We are not cavemen, far from it, though you might be forgiven for thinking we were had you come across us in the days after our arrival, those eighteen short years ago.

But first, in guise of introduction to this account, the first section of which I could not write until ten years after our arrival when, after numerous disappointments, we finally managed to develop a support of sorts for our scribblings (now we have real paper, as you can see), let me tell you something of myself. This, to anchor what you read - of where we lived before, of how we came here, of what we have become - to a real person who experienced everything he here describes. When you find this you will be as distant to us as we are to the people who left us the rock painting of the shaman and the hunters and the ambling reindeer and the women gutting the hares.

\*

My maternal ancestor was Chinese, born in what was then Taiwan, that leaf-shaped island off the coast of China. Her own parents were from Beijing, now, *then* I should say (how difficult it still is to shake off what so recently *was* now) twin capital of the Chinese Union, where the family had lived for generations, as members of the *umma*, followers of the true faith, who refrained from pork and buried their dead within twenty-four hours, as the Koran requires. One of her uncles became a mullah - I have a grainy image of him in his white haji cap. He is holding a young boy in his arms beneath a slowly turning fan on some sunny balcony in a place called Xiang Gang. This is the first Eurasian in the family.

Another relative had been an assistant to Haji Khaled Shi Zizhou, who had translated the Book from Arabic to Chinese. They had worked from nine to noon every day for seven years. And when the printed version was published, he painstakingly wrote it out again in his own calligraphy of big, bold characters for easier study by the elderly faithful. (Does the Book mention my former home? *Al Qahira* it is called in Arabic. Probably not.)

Her husband was British, Scottish more precisely, although he himself was born and brought up in England, some seventy years before disunion. His own father had been born in India, the son of a *Scotch Christian engineer*, as the birth certificate data my father passed on to me quaintly puts it. He spoke Bengali as a child, went to school in a hill town called Darjeeling, which was cooler than Calcutta and, from the photographic record, wore a solar topee whenever he went outside. He returned to his native Scotland at thirteen, left school at fourteen, and served an apprenticeship as a mechanic in a local firm. I have a very small black and white photo of him, spanner in hand, standing next to what looks like a one-man helicopter but in fact is an autogyro, according to fading notes on the back. He mentions the name Juan de la Cierva, with *inventor* in brackets after it. There are no further explanations.

He liked the sea and boats. I have a short, probably true story, he wrote about a yacht caught in a squall. A man falls overboard and is almost drowned because the crew forgot the cardinal rule: *Always keep your eye on the man in the water.* In the drawing which accompanies it, a figure among the waves, weighed down by his waterproofs, raises an arm in supplication as the boat sweeps past him. In the end they spot him and he is saved.

*What took you so long, you bunch of fucking grocers!* he grumbles in relief.

But that was on the human level - someone knows you are in trouble, cares you are in trouble and does something about it. But who cared whether that explosive bloom - 11 billion people - lived or died? No one, and never has. Not even a malignant force, something as *vast, cool and unsympathetic* as Wells' Martians, which, in an act of mischievous cruelty, might have granted them a temporary reprieve for a blink of cosmic time before coldly wiping them out fifty million years later.

There is nothing out there, nothing, just the *infinite and gratuitous awfulness of fluid space,* as a mid-twentieth century writer so perceptively and dismissively described it, long before any living thing - dog, ape or man - had even been there. I realised that a long way into our journey, when Earth was still the palest of pale blue dots. Forgive me. Anyway, he married and moved to England where my great great grandfather was born in the middle of a war, his future, and that of his companion-to-be from the other side of the world, then as unknown as ours still is as we near the end of this second decade of our new existence. We have grown out of their future. What will grow from ours?

*

# **The Settlement**

I don't know when I became aware of it - aware that where I had been born and raised and educated was so different. Was it? It seemed very ordinary to me, to all of us. I went to school with the other children; it was a ten-minute drive in the school bus from where we lived, had lunch at school, always pulses of one kind or another, mushrooms (there always seemed to be basil in it, which I hated), corn on the cob and, in those days, a hand-pollinated peach or apple, and then back home, and homework.

After supper, which was usually vegetable soup thickened with soy and lentils and eaten with wholemeal bread and a salad, we gathered in the living room, sometimes with one or two neighbouring families, for games of chess, or go, or sang songs while I tried to keep up on my recorder. Dad would tell us stories about the pioneers. Some of them had never actually made the journey but had had the ideas which made it possible for others to live there, like Zubrin, the man the settlement we lived in was named after, or Hohmann who worked out the celestial mechanics of it all. Sometimes Mama would get out her brush, by then a wispy shadow of its former bushy self, and she and my sister would practice writing the old language in a tray of finely ground dust. Other times they flicked abacus beads invisibly up and down in the air, racing to find the answer to the sum I had given them.

I read of course. Like every other household we had access to huge libraries. Often I fell asleep like that. Dad would find me in bed, my face all aglow with the lights from the screen and my index finger still propped up against the surround. My dreams, however, were special, always about open spaces - rustling grasslands, humid jungle, a sodden river delta, undulating meadows, old wild wood - and always devoid of any living creature except myself. They were not frightening dreams, just a gentle decaying of my normal sleep trajectory into another layer of mind for a few timeless minutes before some neural delta-vee lifted me back on course into the void of dream-free sleep. Random? Nothing was random we'd been told by Shaw, our chaos teacher in Pre-qual 5, but what the initial conditions for my dreams were was still a mystery, even then.

*

But some days were special.

We first heard the buzzing in the corridors - not the usual beeps and trills and pings which we heard every day but waves of a louder, deeper sound, almost tactile in their intensity. When we got to the assembly point where the bus backed into the lock, the screen was off - no dust storm warnings, no news of new crops, solar flares, or new habitats. Then, in a flurry of crepitation, luminescence flooded the screen and there it was, in close-up, its giant head, miraculous and repulsive in equal measure, filling every single pixel of the three by four metre display. We had known it was coming for weeks - it had been all over the network, on the smaller monitors in the access corridors, and we'd talked about it at school. But it still came as a surprise. We were no longer alone, after more than one hundred and fifty years of solitude.

The head grew smaller as the camera zoomed out, to a long stretch of green and purple which we saw was a clover strip - the clover strip. There was only one. And there, right in the middle, barely visible in long shot, was the bee. It flew over the clover, dropping down here and there to immerse itself in the irresistible sweetness of the flowers before careening off a sudden hardening in the air where the plants gave way to the regolith, the rubble desert stretching to the horizon, forty kilometres away beyond the transparent dome which kept us safe.

The visit to Triple Point was special as well, in an otherwise unspecial existence, as I thought it then. We were to be away for seven nights. There was a lot of excitement at that - and my sister was very jealous but she was too young to go. We'd be sleeping on the rover, in bunks, and the screenie from school said we were all to have a shower before leaving as there would be no washing facilities on board and only limited ones at our destination. The school provided the suits and we had to take all our food as well.

We set off just before dawn. Illuminated by our headlights, frost glittered on the roadside rocks as we pulled away from the lock and headed south down the frozen highway. Behind us, the domes and atria of the Settlement huddled tightly over their crops and still sleeping humans before slowly slipping from view. The outside temp was -85C. The Valley was a thousand kilometres away to the south-west. We had never gone out so far before.

We stowed our gear and watched the dawn come up pink and clear as we ate our breakfast. At nine, just as we were settling down at our screens, Ariella, who was driving, announced an eclipse.

*Here it comes*, she said.

We all rushed to the forward viewing port. She pointed out to the right and by the time we saw it, the fringe of it was on us and over us, silently hurtling across the terrain at hundreds of kilometres per hour. There was no darkening, just a momentary drop in the light, not much longer than a blink, and then less pale sunlight again. Lee, not very seriously, was moaning to himself - he had been looking elsewhere and missed it completely.

We'd all seen recordings of one, an oval shadow ninety kilometres long racing across the landscape as Phobos passed in front of the sun on its seven-and-a-half hour rush around the equator, but never actually been outside when it happened.

*It's going to crash soon,* I remember Zhudi saying. (I always remembered what she said.)

*What do you mean by soon?* Su taunted her, nicely, *Before we get back to Zube?*

*You know what I mean, the thing is decaying. Next year the shadow will be going even faster, not that we'd notice the difference.*

*Yeah, and in fifty million years it will hit the top of the atmosphere and burn up or crash,* Szeto interjected, leaving it to others to decide whether she was being sarcastic or supportive - she wasn't sure what the rest of us thought.

We'd heard all of this in Earth studies. We knew that Phobos was about the same size as the object which hit Earth 65 million years ago, wiping out all the dinosaurs and seventy-five per cent of everything else that was living.

*What a catastrophe!*

I could still hear Alvarez telling us that, hamming up his distressed ecofreak performance more than usual - which told us there was good news round the corner.

*What a break!,* he exclaimed, leaning towards us, his right palm hammering the air three times in emphasis.

*Enter the mammals! That event opened the door for us, blocked one route, opened another, and here we are, so don't knock the rock - mass extinctions are not necessarily bad! They're part of evolution, too.*

We liked that, less aware then than we are now that a similar impact there, at that time, would not have changed anything much, apart from chucking up a bigger amount of ejecta than usual and blowing into space the few remaining molecules of atmosphere the solar wind had missed. A dead planet cannot be made deader.

At twelve we stopped to take a reading. We knew where we were of course; the road, a rock-cleared strip of rego little more than a couple of vehicles wide, was clearly marked on the navilog, but for the class exercise we had to pretend we didn't. The temp was way up, only -5C, and the carbofrost had subbed off hours ago. We suited up, waited for the purge, and then stepped down. Underfoot the duricrust at the side of the road crumbled like biscuit beneath our weight. I worked with Hong, punching in the data as he announced the sextant readings. Wind speed was 80kph, just enough to raise a bit of dust off the surface but in our suits...hardly perceptible. I picked up a chunk of rock and threw it at a boulder about two hundred metres off. Contact! There was a noise of thin cracking as sounds waves clawed their way back through the insubstantial air to where I stood.

Overhead, Deimos glowed palely, an anaemic Venus soberly tracking across the sky from east to west in silent reproach of its duller sibling waywardly chasing its shadow in the opposite direction. Off in the near distance I could see a trio of dust devils twirling drunkenly across the landscape and all around me the criss-crossing tangle of the tracks they and their spent cronies had spun into the dust.

*

*Dong Nan Xi Bei* - East South West North - we knew the bearings, the compass rose, whatever the language, Chinese or English, whatever the order. We knew what a compass was (a south-pointer, the old language called it) and that it was quite useless there. What I didn't know then - and it somehow made our claim to be living there, to be putting down roots, to be starting a new civilization, sound even more hollow in retrospect - was how the simple physical fact of magnetism, that skein of forces which held, still holds, the Earth in its invisible web, had created not only lode stones but cultural facts as well.

We knew no one had lived there before. There were no signs of anything but absence - total, unending, uninterrupted absence. No ochre handprints caught in the sweeping beam of a flashlight quickened the heartbeat of teenage explorers deep within the quiet of a cave; no mysterious edifices, no Great Walls,

11

ziggurats, pyramids, or massive arrays of standing stones, scoured and rounded by erosion, fired the imagination of poets and archaeologists (the Face which late 20th century adepts of life elsewhere had seen on Cydonia was nothing more than an artefact of insufficiently enhanced data - not the beacon some had so wanted it to be). Nothing.

But even if there had been inhabitants at the time when liquid water still existed, without those unfelt lines of force, whatever they might have created would have lapped against a vast zone of absence - no geomancy, no literature of divination, no lodestone spoons, the "ladles of majesty" on their heaven-plates by which emperors could align themselves with the sacred southern direction, no toy facsimiles of men or ships drawn to each other like long lost lovers or propelled apart by the same invisible force, no fighting chessmen used by court magicians to impress their emperors, no metal fishes quiveringly pointing to the poles in their bowl of water, no compass needles balancing on their pin - *here's where we have come from; here's where we are going*, they mutely signed; *the future is ahead, out there, beyond the horizon.*

Here on Earth, magnetism was one of the feedstocks of culture. It was a magical exhalation, a *qi* of wonderful penetratingness from which so much was spun and so much developed. Trivial market day crowd-stoppers, awesome gadgets of imperial power - these were the forerunners of the magnetic compass, and the vertiginous discoveries of how the world was which followed in the wake of its adoption. There, its few feeble wisps would have gone unnoticed.

*

There were twelve of us, all in pairs, waiting to use the sextant and datalogger. There was no other traffic, although we could see the faint tracks of the three or four other vehicles which had come down the road in the years before. The landscape was pretty much as it was at Zube, rock-strewn hematite desert interspersed with low hummocks. Some of the rocks were a couple of metres across but most were much smaller. All were mantled by miniature dunes of dust which had settled out of the air after the dust storm the previous week. As the breeze gusted up to 100kmh, sand on the rock just in front of me sifted off its slope and piled up in a cone at its base.

I could see Xing away to my left, about three hundred metres from the road, half hidden by a big rock. He had gone looking for the proverbial fossil. (We knew there weren't any but ...) My phones hissed.

*Get over here quick!*

He had found something. All the others had turned, herd-like, in response to his call.

*

There was nothing there - nothingness was the name of this place. Even the names we used were imported, tacked on to a topography unleavened by memory, however dim, however reconstructed. They were John Doe names, contingent, arbitrary, barely suffused (for those to whom they still spoke - and they were very few) with the history and culture of another place four hundred million kilometres away at its most

13

distant - Noctis Labyrinthus, Barnard, Elysium Mons, Amazonis Planitia, Valles Marineris, Lyot...

No native memory found its way up through roots, however tenuous and desiccated, to time now. No long-disappeared aborigines, the Monongahela, Qauqaut, Okonee, Kavalan...had charged the land with their names. No ghostly presence, the only reminder of their existence, hung in the air. No thistles thrust their spikes against the air, defiant reincarnations of ancient dead staining the earth beneath their roots, as a poet once described them. There was no overburden of history, no middens, no dark strata of long extinguished ashes, no bones of folk, no folk memories, no folk, period. It was an empty place. Even time seemed not to exist in that endless, undifferentiated duration in which nothing had ever happened, or even started to happen for hundreds of millions of years. There had been no false starts, no mass extinctions, nothing more eventful than a scattering of landslides, unheard, unseen, unfelt. Patches of ragged parachute material were sometimes found, half hidden in sand or snagged on some outcrop of rock, their lettering all but faded away by the UV. An unexposed fold might reveal a Chinese character or two, a broken ring of blue stars, a patch of red and white bars, spokes of a spinning wheel. But we knew they were just relics of early missions from the days before Settlement. They were not from Mars. Nothing came from Mars.

*

Xing was no longer to be seen, though we could hear his breathing. Then his helmet bobbed up behind the rock. With a peremptory, upward flick of his arm he summoned us over. Lewis joined us - he'd stayed back in the rover to check the communications but Xing's gasp of surprise had reached him and Ariella as well. It was the helmet I saw first, half buried in the sand; it was not a kind I recognised. The visor had crazed; exposure had frazzled its reflecting surface into matt patches of green and orange, and the neck seams had perished. A suit glove lay beside it, palm up, the index finger pointing dumbly in my direction above a tapering wind-tail of sand.

Then I saw the body - Xing had found a sleever. He must have chosen a warm day (if it had been that premeditated, which wasn't certain). The temperature would have been a few degrees above zero, maybe even higher. The blood had had plenty of time to flow before the freeze set in. He had even taken his suit off, which would have left him even less time, but there was no sign of panic. The body lay stretched out over a knee-high rock the length of a small table. His cheek lay against it and his arms had reached out to grip, no, to caress the corners - there was nothing aggressive about his posture. He might have been rock solid but there was a softness there, a sense of intimacy which I realised in recollection was almost sexual. It was not a pretty sight - the gases and fluids of his suffocating body had exploded through whatever stood in their way to get to the low pressure beyond the unprotected skin. His eyes were ragged craters of rusty dust and black, deep frozen, blood. From his mouth, half filled with fine rubble, a viscous stream of liquids had oozed across the surface, massed at the edge of the rock and frozen just before the straining bulge could burst down the side. Blood had filled his ear on the sky-side of his face and then overflowed over the front and back of his neck, pinning him in an icy black halter to the rock. He had known what would happen, yet he had gone ahead all the same.

*Likai hongchen,* leaving the red dust, we used to say in Chinese of someone who dies. Here we leave it reluctantly (it comes in many forms), held back by love, of course, but also by the pleasures of the senses - the full smell of wet earth after the rain, the sight of a dawn-dappled sky, of the orange and grey underbelly of a newt, the rustle of aspen leaves glancing into white before a soft breeze, the caress of a catkin across your cheek …so many ordinary pleasures.

There, beyond the Settlement, where red dust was everywhere, there was less patience - it got to you in the end, that continual living at one remove from immediate contact, that enforced modesty which kept you behind plastic and glass, artificially pressurised, wrapped and visored against radiation, touching, breathing, hearing, seeing, through man-made screens and tubes and wires, forever bound by survival protocols, forever inhaling the same dry and savourless air. In the domes or atria it was different of course - you were not right up against it there. You could move around unencumbered, catch the occasional olfactory surprise, pleasant and unpleasant, in a shirt-sleeve environment as they called it (hence the name *sleever*), but even there it took its toll.

Access to the outside was strictly controlled, by common consent; everything was in limited supply which could not be grown or manufactured on base, and even that was not available in abundance. There were no fleets of rovers one vehicle of which you could borrow for a Martian "picnic"; there were about thirty for a population of 3000. Before the impactor a new one or two would come in from Earth every eight years or so, but that was it. Even "my" recorder was number 36 of a batch of one hundred delivered over a generation ago. We had applied for one and been lucky - the computer had randomly allocated it to us, for a five-year period, at the end of which someone else would get it.

Kitchen utensils, furniture, clothes, bedding, medicine, bandages, food, were all very basic and functional but treated with the care accorded to precious stones. Packaging did not exist beyond the most rudimentary requirements of containing otherwise spillable substances. We kept the toothpowder in a plastic tub, refillable at the pharmacenter and rubbed it on with our fingers; soap the same - a viscous, unscented, yellowish glop made from the recycled dead. We were not squeamish out there - bodies were a resource we could not afford not to use, but not for what you might think. Refrigeration was not a problem; that was part of the environment. But our surgical expertise was strictly "frontier" grade - there was very little transplanting, even less gene therapy, and absolutely no nanosurgery. Everything, everybody - our dead, the food scraps of the living, our shit and piss - went into the digester. Out the other end came a rich, odour-free mulch pullulating with bacteria which we dug into the inchoate humus a few decades of waste vegetation from the hydroponic tanks had started to create out of the life-free Martian soil beneath the domes. (I was wrong to say the bee was the first life form - but you knew what I meant; it was the first thing you could actually see.) And gas - methane - to run the generators and power the rovers.

So you couldn't just take off to the outside - vehicles were few, pressure suits even fewer. There were no paramedics on constant standby, no endless supply of blood plasma, or anaesthetics, or antibiotics, no disposable syringes or pre-packaged alcohol swabs and no guaranteed replacement of surgical expertise. If you were outside without authority you were on your own; you were endangering the community. The value of one human body was far less than the cost to the community of the massive outlay required in vehicles, personnel, fuel, oxygen, and skills temporarily reallocated from more important work, all the more so if the rescue bid was unsuccessful. The multiplier effect of failure on Mars rapidly became life-threatening - there was no Plan B; the end of the line was always in sight.

People *locked* from time to time, took off through an airlock - not every week, or even every month but often enough over the years to make it a fact of life. It wasn't easy - most people had no access to the codes and, surprisingly (well, perhaps not so surprising given our circumstances - we were an other-regarding society, puritan in many ways but without the lack of compassion which so often distorts that quality) no one had cared so little about their fellow settlers that they had simply driven a rover through the wall between them and the deceptively unbounded landscape beyond.

But if outside missions were part of your job then you would have access to a code and a vehicle. There

18

were security precautions - authorizations to be obtained, levels of clearance, prioritizations - but no inexhaustible pool, not even a shallow puddle, of people to enforce them. We had not developed to that stage where demand was inevitably met with supply. We couldn't have made a pencil (I had seen just a couple in my life), even with a committee. There was no invisible hand up there - the hand that we worked with was all too visible, and a couple of digits short into the bargain.

It was mainly fragile trust that kept things operating, and when that started to crumble, there were always empathogens. But we used them much less than on Earth where ignorance, swollen populations and the competition for resources had made it much less easy to define the Common Good to the satisfaction of all. There (or rather *here*, as it used to be) the pilot use of pharma-control to end communal conflict, by spraying the stuff from the air or adding it to the water supply, or just making sure that the leading members of both sides were long enough in the Resolution Room to get a brainful of the happy substance, had enemies telling each other overnight how happy they were to be friends, how everyone could share the river or oil or diamond mines or holy sites and why didn't we think about it before the land was littered with mass graves, mines, and the hacked off limbs of innocents. But still there was reluctance to use it across the board. Maybe D-503 was right - why was it wrong to execute one individual murderer but let millions die of preventable starvation, sickness or massacre? The moral maths wasn't quite as simple as Zamyatin's narrator had it - it was good that judicial killing had practically stopped - but you could see what he'd meant.

Respect for Life, Liberty and the Pursuit of the Common Good were the guiding principles the autonomists had come up with. There, without that third term, there would be no Life and no Liberty. There was no question of surrendering ourselves to that land, each one going his individual way, striking out into the unknown, into the unstoried wastes over the horizon. We had cut our entanglement with them (a breach more symbolic than real, given the tenuousness of what was already there) but that land was no more ours than we were its. There the Common Good was a survival protocol, but if you were determined to abuse it, by removing your skills and expertise, you could.

One or two just stepped outside, walked a few steps and then desuited. Others made an expedition of it. *We're going to have a picnic*, they would probably say to the kids, *but it's a secret, so you have to hide in the equipment bins.* The integrity officer would wave the vehicle into the lock - he would think they were going to check the agrotents for damage after the dust storm or clean up the photo panels which kept the pressure pumps going - and they were free. If it was found, the vehicle would be recovered. But if the bodies were nowhere to be seen, there would be no more than a perfunctory search.

And wherever they lay, there they would stay, slowly mounding over with each successive dust season, occasionally softening when the temperature, creeping up over zero, melted their outer surfaces for a few brief hours before plummeting back to the cryogenic levels which would keep them forever there.

I wonder (now that I and the few who came with us and the two we found here are the only people to know about the Settlement) how the future will interpret their remains and whatever else they find out there.

\*

You see how pessimistic I am: an epidemic, a small impact, even one berserk settler would be enough. They are now, more than ever before, completely on their own. For the last time in my lifetime and perhaps that of generations of my descendants, human voices, our own, travelled across that gulf to announce our arrival here, heard them reply some forty minutes later, spoke again, heard them again with the same delay and then, silence. Our receiver had finally failed; the last link was severed.

Was Mars inhabited? By micro-fossils? By man? Or something different but totally unsettling in its similarity to ourselves? Some intelligent kind of ape?

You could see them - a team of perhaps five or six. What, two thousand years later? Maybe sooner. A little awkward in their dual roles as ambassadors of Humanity II (all that flag-and-footprints stuff and stiff horseplay) and scientist explorers. They have no knowledge of mysterious canals, of Flash Gordon's Trip to Mars, of Buck Rogers, of the hostile vision of the planet portrayed in The War of the Worlds, or of the mass hysteria which followed its radio adaptation on Halloween 1938.They have no knowledge of Mars 2 - the first man-made object to crash-land on Mars in 1976, of the Viking and Sojourner missions, which landed there safely before the beginning of the third millennium, of the mapping orbiters and penetrating probes which arrived in its early years, or of Settlement itself.

Maybe they would have a few folk memories (we would be the source), as wispy as those of the cataclysmic flood which purportedly made the Black Sea, from before the time written records started to reappear, but no hard data. The records had all been destroyed, along with the artisanal and industrial infrastructure which made the exercise possible in the first place. Their fly-bys have detected what look like man-made structures - four equally spaced mounds set in a larger sand dune and a grid of lower, dust-covered structures covering some three to four square kilometres in area. For twenty minutes their excitement has propagated through the interplanetary space they spent nine long months to cross.

*Nanhai, Nanhai. This is Tianlong - we have found something.*

All heads in the control room are cocked at exactly the same angle, listening to the faint signals from their headphones. At the water dispenser a technical aide stands, frozen, cup beneath the spout; at the door another figure has halted in mid step, her head thrown back to catch the words form the wall speaker she and everyone else has wanted to hear…

And then the pictures - a close-up of a sandy mound of vaguely humanoid shapes, as though a child, unskilled in modelling, had angrily clumped his clay figures together in frustration at his lack of talent, chucked them aside, and gone on to something else They are part of the landscape, but not an original part. And when they find out, another mystery remains - were they always there? Were they Martians, humans, or something hybrid in between? They will find out later that they are above average in height, with wide chests and spindly limbs, perhaps the result of generations of life in gravity a third that of Earth's, under atmospheric pressure a mere 350 millibars instead of a thousand. Or perhaps just an unusually lanky family - two of the shapes are much smaller. Maybe children. The gravity they know about already but not the pressure, although they will probably read across from their own technology when they finally open up the habitats.

*

We photographed the body and made our way back to the rover. There was less chat than usual. I caught up with Zhudi. We seemed to take to each other although at sixteen we were both pretty inarticulate about the attractions we were starting to feel. I was trying to be blasé about it all but the discovery of the sleever had shaken me as much as everyone else, even though we knew of their existence. The place wasn't littered with them but there were enough to suggest that the pioneering impulse - the *because it's there* syndrome - was weakening with every new generation. The gung-ho starter teams of the first years of Settlement had ignited the imagination of hundreds of applicants with their visions of a planet greening before their very eyes.

They would live under plastic at first, for a few generations at least (so the literature went), and then, as terraforming began to bite and the temperature climbed degree by degree, under a thickening but still unbreathable atmosphere. Plants would survive without protection and humans with only oxygen masks, free of cumbersome pressure suits. Cluster bombs had been released above the poles, covering vast swathes of ice and frozen $CO_2$ in a fine, black, sun-absorbing dust through which gas and water vapour, released from their normal phase by the "warmth" thus generated, could climb into the scraggy martian air and boost the feeble greenhouse effect of the planet's tenuous atmosphere.

As part of the same mission, redundant military rockets strapped together in bunches of five - one to carry the payload, four to lift it on its way - had seeded the upper atmosphere with complex mouthfuls of CFCs. Cost, and a certain uneasiness about the ethics of using substances banned on earth to make a dead planet alive (not to mention polluting the Earth's upper atmosphere with tonnes of toxic rocket fuel in the process), had put a stop to that.

Other schemes were so fraught with imponderables as to stay on the drawing boards, exciting though many people found such radical solutions to the unbendingly inhospitable environment they had yet to experience. Arshuvsky's plan to create a crater fourteen kilometres deep by crashing an asteroid into the Martian surface was one of them: the atmosphere would be the same, so they would still need oxygen, but there would be so much of it above them that they wouldn't need pressure suits or pressurized living quarters. Who would have lasted long in that hole in the ground?

*

I went back to the rover. Far above, the fossil impression of a lizard's tail slowly disintegrated in a patch of bluish cloud drifting across the pale peach sky. Standing on the lower step I ran the vacuum de-duster over my shoes and gloves and did the same for Zhudi before handing her into the cabin. She certainly didn't need any help but let me do it and I felt good that she felt good about it and didn't mind if the others saw.

Lewis did a head count - no one missing. We waited for the pressure to come up and desuited when the green came on. We hung the emus in the locker and then settled down and waited for Lewis to give us some feedback on the datalogging.

On the other side of the rover from Zhudi and I, Szeto Mack was holding out her hand to some of the others.

*Look, but don't touch*, she said, *the oil from your skin will damage it.*

I went over. It was a blue and white square, about 6cm x 6cm, with writing on it. Paper. I had seen some before, a yellowing piece of newsprint with a list of names and temperatures and little symbols - a cloud with rain drops, a cloud with lightening flashes, a full sun, a sun half hidden by cloud - which Grandpa kept by his bed.

*Extra*, Szeto's read. *Sugar-free gum - Made of sorbitol, gum base, mannitol, glycerol, hydrogenated glucose syrup, natural and artificial flavours, aspartame, lecithin, BHT (to maintain freshness), phenylaline - five sticks - Peppermint.*

Everyone got to look - we didn't use paper (to use was to have) though we knew what it was. It must have been handed down through her family - a smuggled item from an early flight. Chewing gum I had never tasted but I had seen some once, in a plastic box. The words *chewing gum* had been carefully scratched onto the surface with a sharp object. It was a pinky-grey wad. It bore two oblong impressions, end to end, separated by a three-millimetre gap - the diastema of whoever had relinquished it. Small fissures had broken up the smooth surface and when you shook the box it rattled. It was 150 years old.

Most families had some relic or other - a toothbrush, a paperclip, a photograph, a small compass which pointed nowhere in particular, a hamster skeleton, a chopstick with red characters, a dusty feather, a pressed flower, even a crumbling sachet of Earth soil. Those were our antiques. There was some trading at first, especially among schoolchildren, but then over the decades this detritus from another world began to take on the significance of a family heirloom - parents hid the stuff away, especially the watches, or lent them to the Wonder-Room, as we grandly called it, for public display. Of course by my time all of the battery-powered ones had stopped, although occasionally someone would get a battery from a rare incomer, before they stopped coming. We would watch as Earth seconds silently ticked their way around the dial or morphed in the window. On Mars we also had sixty minutes to a second and sixty minutes to an hour, but our day was 1.0275 longer than an Earth one, so our units were 1.0275 longer too. Yet even Mars-time watches were few and far between, given only to mission leaders in the early days. When we needed the time we checked it against the computer screen or the displays in public areas. No one had a personal watch they looked at.

\*

By then we were bumping along quite fast and the light was fading. The sun, half the size of the one that earlier today burnt my neck and forearms as I smoked the bees into a new hive, was sinking wanly below the horizon. Sunset there was a technical term - there was no heart-lifting display, no symphony of colour and cloud, no numinous presence - just a pale disk sneaking out of sight, an ailing Sisyphus all too aware that the rock-cracking cold of the Martian night would once again quench his feeble attempts at warming as it had done aeon after aeon after aeon. There was no positive feedback loop there: heat, therefore out-gassing, therefore more greenhouse effect, therefore more heat, therefore more out-gassing, and so on - nothing but an endless back to square one. On the very hottest of rare hot days the temperature might reach 22° C; by night it was down to -90° C, the daytime gain lost to space through the threadbare shroud of $CO_2$ surrounding the planet.

We would be stopping soon for the night. Zhudi had fallen asleep, her head on the bench. Conversation, which had dropped off to the occasional remark after lunch, was picking up again as we approached suppertime. There was a subdued sense of excitement at spending our first night outside. We stopped, right on the road - nothing else would be along. We knew we were one of only three or four vehicles out on the whole planet. One was near the South Pole - Feng's mother was in it, a geo survey of the layered deposits of dust and ice that characterised the area. What a desolate place that was! I had never been there but I knew there was not even the comfort of seeing the two moons. South of 69° latitude Phobos disappeared; south of 82°, Deimos. Not that they gave any light but knowing you could see what the Settlement could see was comforting. And in winter it was even worse - not even the stars could be seen through the cloud cap.

We microed some fonio and dried vegetables and drew our water from the dispenser. Everyone had the same. Bunks had yet to be allocated - I hoped to get next to Zhudi but there was no guarantee. I think Lewis quite liked me but was not sure if he knew about Zhudi and me. He was always busy checking things rather than persons, except as things to be counted. "Paxman", we called him - humans were just elements to be housed and kept in good running order, like the Sitra which made our oxygen or the lithium scrubbers which removed our $CO_2$.

*Free bunking - pick your own*, he said as we were spooning up the last grains of fonio.

*Well, that was nice*, I remember thinking - he recognised us as young adults at last, unlikely to squabble over who got what. Maybe that sleever had set him thinking.

Outside it was completely dark. Stars glowed steadily in the vault above us. In the light from the cabin, prickles of frost sparkled on the road-side rocks and the side of the vehicle. I glanced at the gauge; air temp was already -65° C and falling rapidly. We rejigged the seating to form the bunks, a tier on each side, three high, two deep. Lewis came out, gave us a last look-over, checked the air quality, and then retired forward with Ariella. An experienced paleo-hydrologist, Ariella was to give us the works on the Valley the next morning.

I got my bunk next to Zhudi's, turned to face her and reached out to take her hand in mine. We hadn't kissed yet but that was what I had in mind once the lights went out. I hoped she was thinking the same. Bunks creaked as bodies tried to get comfortable in less place than they were used to back home. Out went the lights. Here and there a red or green pinpoint glowed reassuringly through the dark interior. Life supporting oxygen sussurated quietly through the vents, its soft exhalations interrupted from time to time by the barely audible cracking of a nearby rock or the plangent pinging of the external skin as the intense cold took hold. Overhead, Phobos streaked by for the third time that day, but without a moonbeam to its name. (I would not see Zhudi beneath the Moon till years later when, as we emerged from the new growth of trees onto the low bank around the lake, *the far-reaching singleness of that wide stare* held us transfixed. It was not until then that I realised just how seamlessly that pre-millennium poet had matched word to world. What memorable lines had our two lumpy pillocks ever inspired?)

I put my hand out to touch her face. She didn't recoil but softly trapped my fingers in her hand. I leaned towards her, aware that my bunk was one of six in the same structure and (I couldn't see a thing) kissed the back of my own hand. Zhudi stifled a giggle, and then I felt her lips on mine. More than a peck, less than an invasion - just a soft pressing, but the message was clear: *I like you*, they said. Then they withdrew; her hand patted mine, squeezed my cheek, and she turned over. I rolled over on my back, happier than I could ever have imagined I would be. I lay awake for some time, fantasizing about the future. Where would I be in five years' time? In ten years' time? When I was 45 (my Dad's age)? Then I fell asleep.

I was sitting by a stream beside a stand of giant hogweed. There were hoof prints in the mud at the bottom of the bank and I could smell the stuff baking in the sun. Zhudi was half swimming, half-walking towards me in the chest-high water. Her hair, glistening wet, was knotted above her head. Her shirt clung to her breasts. It was very humid. *Come on in*, she said, in a strange buzz I had never heard her use before. The buzzing got louder. I opened my eyes. Zhudi was next to me, still asleep. It was just getting light. Through the forward partition window I could see Lewis. The buzzing stopped, he smiled at me, pointed to the two sets of bunks and signalled he wanted me to get people up.

By six-thirty we had breakfasted - grains and dried fruit with a helping of soy milk which we had to rehydrate ourselves, and a fusion of mint. The tea (it wasn't tea but that's what we called it) was warm rather than hot. The water had boiled okay when we made it but under that pressure hardly burnt your lips. Some rovers were fitted with pressure pans, but not ours. Outside there was no liquid water - anywhere. Water in its liquid state had last existed hundreds of millions of years ago. We had arrived too late. Now the only water was the chemically bonded stuff in the soil, the ice deposits at the poles and the gravelly reservoirs in the permafrost, a frozen reminder of a time when white hot magma deep within the planet had burst up through it and briefly melted its captive liquid.

Floods more gigantic than anything the solar system has seen since swept across the planet at hundreds of kilometres an hour, changing its face forever. They left riverbeds, run-off channels, plains of boulders pushed hither and thither by raging currents, teardrop islands, and broken-rimmed craters. But not a drop of liquid water, flowing or still, salty or fresh, not even a muddy slurry, survived to our time.

Over the endless millennia of Martian existence the atmospheric pressure had dropped millibar by millibar to a level at which water, as a liquid, could no longer exist. We got a cup of barely hot tea in the rover; outside, if the temperature was above freezing, a pan of water would have emptied before we had even started to heat it, boiling off into gas before our eyes. On "hot" days no puddles formed from melting ice - the stuff simply missed a phase, changing from ice to gas in one quick step…except at our destination, and even then that would depend.

The only real body of water Ariella, our paleohydrologist, had ever seen in her life was the swimming pool back at Zube; otherwise she had to make do with the breathtaking visions of *Mars with hydrosphere* which the Nasa school of painting had turned out by the dozen before Mars fatigue set in and terraforming had been abandoned.

Funny, there is one thing I miss when I think about it - swimming, or rather fooling around in water. Here I weigh sixty-five kilos. (I was seventy on arrival but physically the extra weight takes it out of you.) But out there I was a mere twenty-seven kilos. Not that we swam much - time was strictly rationed so that everyone could get a go. The pool was nothing special either, just a scooped out patch of rego coated with our own base-made sealant, which happened to be brown. It was more a waterhole than one of those shimmering sharp-edged rectangles of blue and white tile that came up on my screen when I entered the word "swimming pool". But when we pushed off from the bottom we came out of the water like dolphins, not quite standing on our tails as they do, but right out to our ankles, before falling back in a flurry of spray which rained down, icy cold, from the dome several metres above. Here, three times as heavy, I feel Earth's restraining hand whenever I try the same.

*Stay!* It says, with an authority I cannot gainsay.

\*

We trundled on across the plain; spent another night on the road (another kiss from Zhudi), and by the beginning of the third day had left the dunes and softer contours of Chryse behind us. The road we were on was less a road than a vaguely defined track which the first explorers had roughly cleared of its larger rocks. The landscape was changing as well; we had crossed the equator. The badlands had begun - a hemisphere of cratered highlands and deep geologic wounds unlike anything to the north of us. We could no longer see the horizon. We were in chaotic terrain where huge chunks of rock had thudded down higgledy piggledy into the rego as though tipped from some giant's sack. Under their frigid overhangs, where the sun never penetrated, we could see rubble coated with the frost which had set in millions of years ago when the planet last shifted on its axis. Tortuously twisted corridors ran - stumbled might be a better word - through the debris on either side of us and we knew from the downward slope of the road ahead and our slower speed that we were entering a new and hazardous world.

Once there had been movement there - hundreds of square kilometres of the plain we had crossed had tumbled into the void as faults opened abruptly beneath it. The still living planet, racked by the seething magma below its crust, had spewed out its burning innards, purging itself of its excessive heat in successively weaker heaves and then, as though exhausted by its efforts, slumped back to await the end, its skin cracking and bursting in the process. Through fathomless stretches of deep time - Noachian, Hesperian, Amazonian - its core grew quieter and quieter as whatever heat remaining ebbed slowly away. Here and there pockets of magma survived, erupting through the crust in great volcanic bursts.

But death was setting in and with it, the irresistible grip of cold. Yet the monuments to its death throes were many. The mighty Mons Olympus was one, a towering volcano to the west-north-west of us. Surrounded by cliffs six kilometres high, it rose up from its vast base to touch the fringes of space, 24 kilometres above. It was higher and bigger than any volcano on Earth. Our destination - The Valley, or Marineris to give it its official name - was another.

*

Lewis told us to check our seatbelts. We may not have weighed much out there but an unrestrained 20 kilogram-human could knock out an instrument panel if we ran into something, even at 20kmh, and if anybody damaged themselves in the process we might have had to go back. There was electricity where we were going but no expertise in facial reconstruction, no more than there was back in Zube.

We were all leaning forward as we dropped deeper and deeper below datum. Here I should explain that as there was no sea on Mars, not in our day at least, there was also no sea level. But we had to use something as a reference point to plot the extremes of Martian topography. (Earth, by comparison, was as smooth as a slightly chipped billiard ball. I have yet to touch one but I believe this line I once read conjures up the right image). The Settlement was the obvious choice - that was datum, and we could measure how far above or below datum we were. One useful indication of where you were with reference to datum was atmospheric pressure. That changed of course with the seasons. When it was "hot" in the northern summer, frozen $CO_2$ subbed off the pole and entered the atmosphere, so the pressure went up, for a while, and then went down again as winter approached and the pole re-adsorbed the gas it had released in the summer. But if you knew the season you could make adjustments for that. Same thing at the South Pole, except more so. This yearly (by that I mean, of course, two Earth years) shuttling of gases from one phase to another pumped thirty percent more $CO_2$ into the air in summer and then froze it out again in winter. But still you couldn't breathe the stuff.

And the more Mars tilted on its axis and exposed its poles to the sun, the more gas there would be. Hence the terraformers' dream (another one!): every 25,000 years at maximum obliquity, when Mars tilts the most, all the frozen ice, the wet stuff and the dry stuff, would sub off, pushing the temperature and pressure up to less hostile but still daunting levels. But *you can't tell a terraformer anything*, as we used to say of anyone stubbornly refusing to face the facts. Without life - teeming, pullulating, omnipresent life, not man or mammals or fishes or birds, but the microscopic stuff, the fungi, the algae, the bacteria - there would be no stability in whatever short-lived conditions technology conned you into creating. It was not a question of "add water, sunlight, and stir with a lightning bolt", a list of ingredients and a suitable receptacle - we could no more have turned Mars into a habitat and filled it with life than we could a gas giant like Jupiter or Saturn.

Already in the pre-millennium Hamilton and Lenton had put paid to that simplistic notion. (*Farting into space,* we called it) It was they who had uncovered the link between the survival strategies of microscopic ocean algae and cloud formation. The biosphere was more than cat fur, more than a cosmetic wrap. Earth was indeed Gaia, a super-organism. And just as Adam Smith's selfish businessmen, working for no other goal than their own enrichment, created the conditions whereby society as a whole became richer, tiny organisms a trillion times smaller than Earth, whose only end was their own dispersal and survival, contributed to cloud formation, by rising into the air in bubbles of self-produced gas. Blocking and unblocking the sun, their clouds regulated the climate like a planetary thermostat, thinning out when it got cold, thickening up when it got warm. Not for our benefit, but we do benefit. Just as we benefit from earthworms, who happen to make agriculture possible, but don't exist to do so. Dinophytes, haptophytes, nematodes - these were the life-forms which counted, not us, with our arrogant alchemist's dream of puffing the *qi* of life into the barren wastes of Mars. It was a tonne of Earth earth which got us started on Mars; another tonne of the stuff had been our emergency rations for here on Earth, if Lovelock and Margulis had got it wrong and the very last spore, the very last bacterium, had in fact been extinguished.

Back at Zube, outside the habitats, the pressure averaged a tiny 5.8 millibars - as feeble as the pressure we had met more than thirty years later as we buffeted our way through the fringes of Earth's atmosphere to the 1000-millibar embrace of her life-given, life-giving gases, forty kilometres below.

*

We had been in the rover for almost sixty hours and were going to be in it for another sixty at least before we got back home and all of us were getting a bit restless. Lewis had promised us an eva before sundown and it was already approaching 1600. We'd had a presentation from Ariella about the origins of chaotic terrain, a brief description of how the Valley had been formed, and instructions from both of them on what we were going to do at the next suit-up.

At last, just on 1600, we stopped, broke out the suits and, as usual, waited. (Here I never have to wait - I just go out, a simple process which still fills me with the innocent wonder I felt when I opened the hatch that very first day and breathed in the sweet exhalations of Gaia. In fact not so sweet, as we later discovered, when the wind was blowing across some recent landslip, but compared to the increasingly foul air on board, a bouquet for the lungs.) The cabin pressure dropped, the door opened and we clambered down. Instead of broken biscuit underfoot we had loose, ankle-twisting rubble and all around us the looming shapes of rocks bigger than any we had seen before. The shadows were lengthening and soon the sun would be gone.

Looking up I could see both moons; Deimos, at that time of day, a pale nugget of light cautiously tracking westward 20,000 km. above us and Phobos, bigger but even paler, cruising swiftly eastward a mere 6000 km. above our heads. As I watched, it disappeared, rubbed out by Mar's shadow. As kids we would bet on whether it would make it across the sky; usually it didn't, except for a few shadow-free days in summer and winter, and when we learnt about them, we stopped. In time, short by cosmic standards, we knew the one would drift off into the wastes beyond Jupiter, the other smack into what we loyally still called home. Then the emptiness would be complete. In class we had studied the report of the first, and last, survey of Phobos. One image had stuck in my mind - from the thigh-deep dust-swamps of the satellite the huge red disk of Mars filled almost half the sky.

There were three pressure gauges. Lewis had laid them out on a chest-high ledge of rock. There were signs that we were not the first there; fractured slabs bore the traces of drilling and on an upright piece placed atop a small cairn there was a neatly chiselled inscription:

$2^{nd}$ *Paleo-Survey, May 2029.*

Below it, much less neatly, someone had added:

*PS. ALH84001 sucks!*

I'd forgotten the reference - Zhudi hadn't, and lost no time in reminding me. ALH84001 was a 4.5 billion year old lump of orthopyroxene. Earth scientists had found it in the Antarctic ice over two hundred years ago. Some time back something big had hit Mars so hard that bits of it had been blasted into space and "Al" was one of them. It had taken the scenic route to Earth, long enough for cosmogenically produced particles (*That means coming from space,* Zhudi had irritatingly explained – I did know the word, though isotope geology was not my strongest subject) to transform some of its nuclei into helium 3, neon 21 and argon 38, which otherwise don't exist. They showed it had been out there for 16 million years before falling to Earth a mere 13, 000 years ago.

*So what has that has that got to do with fossils?* I asked, curious to know but nervous about being lectured at again with the others listening in.

*Vestiges of microbial life*!, she replied, in the way you might say *Beancurd* in answer to a toddler's question about what the moons were made of.

*You're kidding - I thought you were being serious. They didn't believe that, did they?*

*Listen, people who believed there was a face on Cydonia, that people had been abducted by aliens and that there is life after death, will believe anything. The thing did have tiny ovoids and tubes in it, like some kind of nanobacteria, but, you know, so did a lot of other rocks which no one believed for a moment were bearers of fossilized remains. There was a lot of controversy, a lot of people extrapolating away* (she used that word a lot) *from what they had found on earth, you know, extremophiles - all these cute little* *nanobes way down in the polar ice or steaming their butts off around some ocean vent. If they are here they might be there as well, but they hadn't been there, you know, I mean **here**, yet. I guess whoever wrote this had had enough of looking under rocks and scrutinising core samples and finding nothing.*

Two or three of the others had stopped to listen - her voice was like that, full of authority even then, despite the teenage lingo. We heard it again on the way here - she was mission leader - when it looked like Xing was not going to make it all the way.

But at least I found something. It was under a flattish, palm-sized piece of rock which years of dust and frost had sealed into the cavity it was covering. I hammered it loose, not really expecting anything. In the hacked out space beneath lay a piece of metal. It was round, about two centimetres across and a couple of millimetres thick. The circumference was wavy. On one side there were two figures in loose-fitting clothes prancing around between a 19 and a 97. There was a small 2 at the top. On the other, a five-petalled bloom. Above it I could read the Chinese characters *Xiang Gang*, and the English words *Hong Kong*.

I knew what it was of course, a coin, though we didn't use them. But the date puzzled me. It was already 32 years old when it came here. It must have been something whoever had put there had deliberately brought with him to leave behind.

He would have known the chances of its being discovered were remote - the boulder he had chosen wasn't marked in any particular way. Had he written the inscription as well? Did that crudity of expression hide a more fragile sensitivity? He knew the big

39

excitement was not for them - finding fossils was a dead end-mission; they probably knew it already. But finding a coin under a rock in a place like that - now that was an SPL - a Small Pleasure of Life, as my father would remark after some trivial but charged event, like the word *Dad,* now without the *dy* at the end, uttered by my own rapidly growing son (who still likes to hold my hand), or the warmth of his sister's small fingers on my nose. I hoped he had imagined this moment - he would have had no idea who could have found it, but he knew that whenever it happened the two of us would be intimately linked. I felt it as soon as I saw the coin, an entanglement as inseparable as the one which binds photon to photon, no matter what gulf of intergalactic space lies between them.

\*

Ground pressure at Zube the day we left had been 5.5mb. But since crossing the equator we had been going down and when we stopped that day we were already 2000 metres lower. It was late in the afternoon but even then we were getting readings of 7.8mb; at noon it would have been higher still. Yet it was still too cold to see what we had come so far to see - that would have to wait for the next day. Our destination was 5500 metres below datum. There, noon temperatures were above zero for at least a couple of hours in the day.

We were jumping around a bit - everyone was feeling the cold despite the thermal protection we were wearing - but games were out; it was too dangerous. We carried adhesive tape on our waist belts for emergency rips, but any activity which brought them about was strictly discouraged. Not that we needed dissuading - the sleever's exploded corpse was reminder enough of what happened if you didn't get a patch on quick enough. Chucking stones was allowed. You set up a pile and then tried to knock it down. There would be a puff of dust as you made contact but hardly any noise, and what noise you did hear came to you through your suit and your helmet. There, even when you were outside, you were still always inside, trapped by the technology which ruled your existence.

We looked around a bit more - you always hoped to find something, even if only a piece of discarded equipment. But nothing was wasted there, even the first Lander was almost cannibalised before whatever team had had it in for that quasi-sacred piece of hardware was persuaded to make do with some other jury rig until the next flight came in, and leave the Viking in peace. The site had been ringed with small boulders and the vehicle itself periodically air-hosed down. But that was decades ago. It was still there of course, but half-buried in dust and the stone circle had turned into a lumpy ring of sand. We had visited a couple of times. By then we had been autonomous for seventy years and it was no longer an icon, just a piece of hardware we vaguely knew about.

There was a whistle from the rover - time to get back. I remember passing my gloved hand quickly across a slab of rock. It was leaning back about 30° so it was free of dust except for the stuff in the erosion flukes. With the sharp end of my rock hammer I hurriedly inscribed the characters of my name - *Han Dengqin* - and the year, month and day, *2186/9/42* By the time I had finished the whistle had sounded again and I could see Lewis standing, arms akimbo, in irritated instructor mode at the bottom of the steps - they couldn't start desuiting until I was back on board. I went to blow the dust off my work, but no sooner had I rounded my lips to do so than I realised I was wasting my breath.

*

It was the last night of the outward trip. We had driven for another three hours, down all the time, and were looking forward to stopping. Our itinerary had taken us out of the chaotic terrain and onto the smoother surface of a massive land slump which provided the essential bridge between the landscape of broken rocks behind us and Triple Point. A vast debris apron - you could still see the ragged hem where a canyon-side of avalanching rego had finally run out of momentum tens of millions of years before - let us precipitously down through a series of man-made chicanes to the floor of the Valley two thousand metres below.

Once on the incline we could not have stopped; there was always the possibility of further movement (so we were told) but it was hard to imagine what might have caused it. Tectonism had long died out, the shifting plates had stilled, and the hot spots had spluttered their last. Impacts might have, but at that time they were about as present in our minds as a sparkling brook round the next outcrop of rock or a shower of rain. (At that time the full impact, to coin a phrase, of what had happened to Earth had yet to send its shockwaves through our young minds.)

At 1930 we stopped. It was quite dark already. Outside pressure was 8.47mb. Above us we had another 3000 metres of atmosphere and the weight was beginning to show. We'd be down another 1000 metres the next day and chances of ideal conditions at Triple Point were good.

What did we talk about those days? Certainly not always our project. Our brains were stuffed with the terminology and concepts of magmatics, stratigraphy, paleo-hydrography, geochronology, isotope geology, celestial mechanics, crater formation, non-linear dynamics and even the more humble vocabulary of biogas digesters, habitat integrity and agro-plant design, but we didn't feel ourselves different as a result.

We had been brought up with all that because of where we were. But, as I explained, where we were was not something we particularly reflected on. Yes, we knew about Earth as people in Asia had known about the golden pavements of China and America. But that didn't make your daily experience of life special in any way. They knew it was better over there, but they weren't over there - they were in their own here and now, and if an occasional dream or flight of fancy suddenly caught them looking back with new eyes at what they had always been, it was just that, occasional, and the overpowering presence of the quotidien quickly nipped in the bud whatever inkling of the other had started to germinate. We talked about what teenagers the world over (strange that expression, now) talked about: everything and nothing.

Our life was not intolerable - no one starved, no one was illiterate, no one was excluded or marginalised. We were all empowered to direct our own affairs. Our habitats were clean and uncluttered but hardly the sleek, garden-city vistas beloved of the Nasa school of painting, more like tidyish farmyards, minus the animals. We lived in a world of strange contrasts (again, I didn't think them strange then): the high technology of an electronic information society which gave me access to the Earth's libraries from my bedside cohabiting with surgical techniques which would have been dated even on early 22nd century Earth.

We had had, very infrequently, rockets to take a handful of us to Earth and enough fuel and food to keep us alive for the journey, but at home we pushed ourselves over the freezepaths on crude iceboards. I was sixteen at the time of our Triple Point trip and already into the habit of stroking the sparse beard which had started to sprout around my jawline - there were no razors. Occasionally one might see a clean-shaven face, stoically bearing the nicks of a home-made cut-throat, but hirsuteness was the norm for men. Hair, when it was cut, was cropped to the skull, and our clothes were functional - smocks and slacks for men and women alike and little else to distinguish one Settler from another. If you were cold you put on more of the same, quilted with your own hair or your companion's. Well-patched Earth clothes, remnants of earlier wardrobes in the first years of Settlement, had long since been consigned to a digester.

Pharmaceuticals were a different matter; we had plenty of them - a million pills and phials was just a fraction of a rocket's payload. Sartorially our women were drab (as were our men, despite the coquetry both sexes displayed, from very meagre resources, to personalise their garb). But their unsophisticated clothing, reminiscent of some 19th century experiment in egalitarian living, hid female physiologies free of monthly cycles and the mental and physical impact of menopause.

\*

When I woke the next day the light was different; a dull haar, almost impenetrable to the feeble rays of a half-sized sun, had settled over the site. Subdued light sifted into the cabin where my classmates were beginning to stir. I got up as softly as I could, not wishing to shake the others awake, and looked out of the port. The towering wall of the Valley, which I knew to be only a few hundred metres off, was quite invisible. I could hardly make out the ground itself, just a metre or so away. If only I could have opened the hatch and stood there, suit-less, mask-less, breathed in the rapt silence of that morning, jumped down to the damp soil and waited for…what? An annunciation? No, something simpler: a slowly recomposing landscape of low hills, trees in silhouette along their crest, the caw of a crow, a distant bark, the curve of a beach way down below and the faint sound of waves and wheeling gulls and, up above, the huge, orange disk of the sun booming silently out of a blue, blue sky.

\*

We had another two hours' drive westwards to Triple Point. The mist had disappeared by the time breakfast was over and we could see where we were. The Valley itself was disappointing. Yes, the cliff was higher than anything we had ever seen before around Zube but when you were in it, it was less than awe-inspiring, despite the statistics. Ariella had told us all about canyons, the ones on Earth - the Colca, in a place called Peru, over 2000 metres deep, the Yarlung, on the borders of the old country, twice as deep again, and the Grand Canyon, a mere 1000 metres or so, God's joke on the creationists.

There, we were already lower than the deepest of them, and set to go lower still. We tried to be impressed by her figures - The Valley was 5000 kilometres long, six kilometres deep at its lowest point and 700 kilometres at it widest. And unlike Earth canyons, no river ever ran through it. It had been shaped a bit here and there by ancient flood waters and gouging slurries of carbo-snow, but no flow of water or ice, however powerful, could have inflicted that great gash on the planet's face. The planet's crust had ripped open, unable to withstand the onslaught from below, and remained open, like a wound deep-frozen before it could heal. But it was difficult to gaze in awe at something so vast you could only appreciate it when you were already off the planet. It was too big for any ground-based human observer; it was a small planet's act of bravado.

Mars is half the size of Earth - the horizon is twice as close - but this particular feature was an in-your-face challenge to the moderation of earthly topography. *Keep your distance,* it seemed to be saying, *the view is better.* Many years later we all gasped when we saw the Valley in its totality, as Mars spun smaller and smaller behind us. Apart from the poles and the cloud-filled maw of Hellas, it was the last feature to remain visible before distance finally shrank our home to an undifferentiated rusty disk that I could blot out with my thumb.

*

Up ahead we could see the base tower. We had reached Triple Point. There we would have more space to move around. We'd brought a ball with us so we could get some exercise without fear of ripping our suits. It was coming up to 0830 and we were all more than ready to leave the rover. Lewis let off a few blasts of the whistle as we drove down the slope below the berm to the lock. He knew the place was unmanned at that time but arriving safely was a relief, even if there was no welcoming party.

Except in the domes, with their protective transparent shield, all other locations were cut-and-cover constructions, shielded from normal radiation by a two-metre layer of soil which also kept the pressurized air from bursting through to the surface. Bricks were used to line the excavations and build the roof vaults. We lived in the $22^{nd}$ century but for sub-surface habs used Roman building techniques inherited from before the first.

There was no vehicle lock and so we all had to suit up, get down, get into the lock, wait for pressure, and then desuit. The lights were on, it was warm, the air smelt fresh, and there was a basket ball court in one corner and a running track round the periphery. There was no running water but there was water - some liquid, in the warmed pits, some frozen in reservoirs, which could be warmed *in situ* or cut out with ice picks if the other stuff ran out. So no problem for a drink or rehydration or even a limited cat-lick. Lewis had detailed Zhudi and myself to get some tea on, which we did, in the galley next to the main chamber. Plaited stalks pulled her hair neatly back from her face; strung on a single strand of copper wire, a cloudy green pear-drop of polished olivine enhanced the elegance of her long neck. It was the first time we had been together out of sight of the others since the trip started.

We sort of nuzzled shoulders to let each other know we enjoyed the proximity, unsuspecting then that some years into the future we would have a world all to ourselves in the most literal meaning of the word - but also a period of confinement before it which made the restrictions of Settlement life seem paradise in comparison.

Outside the galley we could hear excited shouts as our classmates explored the base. Through the anti-UV louvre just below the ceiling, luke-warm sunlight crept slowly down the wall opposite as midday approached. I could see the dusty base of the generator tower. From the wind gauge I knew that 80 metres above us its twin blades were turning slowly in the 95kmh breeze. I also knew that it was the feeble push of that dust-dry breath, and nothing else, which was keeping us alive.

*Hurry up in there,* I heard Ariella shout impatiently. I thrust a fistful of mint leaves into the pot and poured on the water. Everyone had their own mugs, and powdered soy milk if they wanted it white, so it was an easy job. We went out and put down the tea. The chairs round the table, itself in brick, were immovable brick bucket-seats, still quite rough after several decades of infrequent use. Ariella was at the screen, adjusting the brightness and adding some figures to the graph. That was what we had come all that way for.

We were restless at having to sit down again so soon after our arrival but we liked Ariella and our grumbling was good-natured.

On the wall opposite me someone had carved a landscape into the brickwork. It must have taken ages; it was no night-time prank. We were looking down a river which ran between high pinnacles of rock scattered on either side as far as the eye could see. One was pierced by a large hole two-thirds of the way up. Here and there a small creature - they looked like goats - clung to their sides. On the river itself a slender bamboo raft drifted in the current, its owner busy with a large bird holding a fish in its beak. There was a wicker basket by his foot, already half full. This more detailed scene, like the goats, had been picked out in black.

*Qing zhou yi guo man zhong shan.*

A line from a Tang dynasty poem my Grandmother had taught me came into my head:

*My little craft has passed ten thousand peaks.*

But I remembered it was monkeys on the banks, not goats, and they never stopped chattering for a second - *Liang an yuan sheng ti bu zhu* - all the way from Bodi Town to Jiang Cheng. And she always added:

*And Li Bai wrote that almost fifteen hundred years ago and we can still read it today.*

We had so little texture in our lives that any departure from unalleviated brickwork was a treat, to

49

me at least. Even a strip of lettuce plants was a gulp of oxygen to my, as I later realised, colour-starved eyes. Gazing through the plastic which separated my shirt-sleeve environment from a $CO_2$-rich agrodome, I would drench myself in that crisp green light to flush away the ochre remanence of a day outside. At home I would gaze at the eggplants and peppers, an eye-fest of pulpy black holes and supernovas in imploding purple and exploding yellow, right there on the galley table. Vegetables, leaves, legumes, fruits, gourds - they were the only palette we had. I had seen a funny painting once on the screen - an arrangement of vegetables and fruits the shape of a man's face. Actually, there were four pictures - Spring, Summer, Autumn, Winter, and all different. The pictures themselves had turned brown with age, but that had set me off. I cut up bits and pieces of peel and skin and arranged them in scenes. They glowed with vitality for the first day or two then faded, or rather became less strident as they dried, and then I realised I could mix the two, the glowing colours of fresh fruit and succulent leaves and the subtler, low-key tones of the dried variety. I wasn't an innovator of course (that was one of our few art forms) but at that time I didn't know it. Beans were another source - dried they could be laid out in swirling patterns of red, white, brown and orange, or ground to different coloured pastes...

*Right,* said Ariella, bringing me back on trajectory, *Triple Point - the only conditions under which ice, liquid water, and water vapour can coexist, and here we have them, or at least I hope so. The pressure is just right and the temperature is just a couple of degrees shy of zero. By midday we should be able to see what we have come all this way to see - liquid water on the surface of Mars.*

She referred to the screen, wrote in the curves for Earth and for what might have been, in some fathomless abyss of deep time, a curve for Mars.

*So you are not going to see this on Olympus Mons.* (Listening to her it suddenly came to me that the vertical distance between where we were then and the top of Olympus was over 30 kilometres.)

*For one thing the temperature is too low - we've got today's. It's already -76° up there, always below freezing, and for another, the pressure is practically non-existent. Look at this: 1.2mb, and that's not even at the summit. But down here, near the bottom of the Valley, we have a column of air 5500 metres higher than at Zube. And higher means, Rodriguez?*

*Heavier,* Rod replied.

*Right, heavier, so more pressure, at least 9.57mb, well above the minimum 6.1mb we need. And we have equatorial sunlight streaming down to a relatively sheltered side canyon, which should push the temp up to above zero. But we'll have to be quick. If we see water it will be gone pretty soon - the ambient air pressure is dry $CO_2$, not water vapour, as you well know, and evaporation will ensure it doesn't linger. So suit up. Let's go.*

It wasn't as though we had never seen water, but the prospect of actually coming across the stuff outside did have a certain fascination. Or was it just being "outside" which was the attraction? We suited up, squeezed into the lock again and waited for the green. The site was a few hundred metres over on our left.

We were about 100 metres from a high wall but in this region of the Valley side canyons were everywhere.

*Temp is now 5° and climbing*, Ariella announced.

I was actually beginning to feel quite warm. The climb up the berm road from the base was a steep one, even in that low gravity. There were twelve of us plus the two adults. Somewhere away to the south of us, Feng's mother and her team would be busy checking cores; elsewhere, maybe two or three other teams mapping the extent of a field of evaporites, and back at Zube the remaining 2980-odd settlers, and that was it. Just 3000 people on 144 million square kilometres (a bigger land mass than Earth's), and a population density of 0.0000268 persons per square kilometre. Martian real estate had not taken off.

*

As we moved along the wall to the side canyon - really a very small one, given the sheer exaggeration of the land forms in that part of the planet - I was suddenly overcome with a feeling that my future was already past. I saw myself as Lewis, leading the way for a party of teenagers just like us on the annual trip to Triple Point, as fixed a part of the Settlement calendar as knee-breaking pollination parties, digester dig-days, or the frosting and subbing of the poles.

Then what? A sedentary job at Zube while children of my own went out on trips, graduated, became mission leaders, led other teenagers on trips, specialized in some *ology* or other, collated data, tired, taught a little school perhaps, spent more and more time at home, and then died, of old age usually, with the sound of small children in their ears. End of one cycle, start of another, and so on and on for ever? I remembered the closing lines of a poem I'd come across, their enunciation of a simple energising truth, stark but compelling, and one which spoke then, as it still speaks, to my condition:

*Dead, we become the lumber of the world*
*And to that mass of matter shall be swept,*
*Where things destroyed, with things unborn, are kept.*

Zhudi gave me a jab, a hard one, as though the last of a series of softer ones which I hadn't registered.

*Where have you been?* she asked.

*I thought your phones had gone. Like walking with a zombie.*

I didn't reply right away. Another jab.

*I want out*, I said.

She grabbed my wrist and leant over it to check the read-out to see if I was low on ox or breathing too much of my own $CO_2$.

*Hey*, she said, *cut it out - we'll be back at base soon, and then you can get out.*

She thought I had sleever fever.

*No, not out of my suit, I mean out of here, off here, away from here, somewhere else.*

Then she understood me.

*Earth?*

We were standing nose to nose, or would have been if there hadn't been eight centimetres of helmet between us. I could just see her eyes through the darkened visor. She held both my wrists in her gloved hands. I wanted to throw my head back and smash through her mask. I saw it happening in slowmo - shards of darkened plastic tumbling in the air, locks of her hair rising and falling and twisting, and her mouth, wide open in laughter, yawing and pitching towards my own, till our lips met in the soundless contact of a space docking.

*Yes, Earth!* I screamed, so loud it tripped the rescue circuit, bringing everyone else in on our chat.

I saw Lewis and the others turning and move towards us.

*He's okay*, Zhudi reassured them, *just a touch of the sleevies.*

Lewis got me to sit down on a rock, checked my read-out and put his arm round my shoulder.

*Yeah, bit of shock that bloke we saw. But you know, he wouldn't have suffered, and in those days he'd be living in one of those tuna cans they used to have, not a base like Zube. So you'll be alright.*

He got up, pulling me up with him, and walked over to the others.

*You stay with him, Zhudi,* I heard him say over his shoulder. I was okay.

\*

Two years before that Earth for me had been no more than a neat little nick at the edge of the solar disk. We'd watched, a little fidgety at that age, as the nick turned into a black dot, traversed the sun and, as unhurriedly as it had begun, breached its other edge and then disappeared. It would come again a hundred years later.

We had seen Earth plenty of times, at that time an unprepossessing dot in the night sky, but there was something special about a transit. Some people would never even see one if they were born just after it. My grandmother remembered her parents speaking about the last one but died before she could see her own. Only one old woman, we were told, had ever seen two, and she had died aged 115, just a few days later.

*Ri-shi* was the name in the old language - eating the sun. But there the sun shone palely on, indifferent to the tiny shadow of distant Earth crossing its small face every one hundred years; indifferent even to the larger shadows cast so frequently on its cold fire by our two scurrying moonlets. For even together, as happened quite often, they covered only a third of the disk.

There, there was no ghostly darkening, no unnatural silence as night turned to day and birds fell silent - just a reminder of how far away...we were? They were? Were they outer space or we? Were we hundreds of millions of kilometres from them or they from us...? Where did that first million start - their end or ours? At that time I couldn't have cared less but then, a couple of years later, it began.

My dreams I told you about, and all that late-night reading. Most of the time I was okay, happy with my life, looking forward to the future, to leaving school, building up an expertise, getting assigned to a team, leading one myself, collecting the data, analysing it, sending it back and starting over again with a new mission. I said at the start you might have mistaken us for cavemen. Well, we weren't, but we were hunter gatherers. That was the basis of our autonomy. Earth had wanted the data - less to explore Mars (we were there already), more to understand Earth. And it was cheaper that way. Governments could no longer afford the capital, not even the prize money it had offered for private ventures to get out there and start importing whatever they could find. Two spectacular disasters had put paid to that. Relatives had sued the companies; the companies had sued the prize-givers, and the prize-givers had counter-sued. And in the meantime 11 billion people had been trying to invent fusion power, combat rising sea levels, reinvent the bee, and get enough water - from other desperate users - to stay alive.

We lived in a wilderness, but it was a peaceful one. And they needed us more than we needed them. And when they no longer did, we continued - what else was there to do? We were inured to hardship, to making do, to being part of a community of like-minded individuals brought together in a fellowship which even the most self-regarding or self-contained amongst us recognised as the condition for our joint survival. We were all kindred. In return, every six or eight years, a ship would land, with some of what we wanted, and even space for people to return. Usually, incoming vessels were unmanned but always fitted out for habitation, and enough nuclear fuel for a five-year trip if things went wrong. But few went. And then it stopped, the last ship arriving from a world nine months dead, like a still-born child delivered from its dying mother. We lived in a light world and our bodies were ill-adapted to coping with Earth's gravity, 70% stronger than our own. It was not necessarily a death sentence, but a Settler's cardiovascular system worked overtime under its new load. And since that one early epidemic we had allowed no one back - our immune systems were fragile and one alien (yes, alien!) bacteria could wipe us out in a month.

\*

We'd come up over a incline and there they were! Thirty or forty of them, some about a metre and a half long, others little larger than a hand - a scattering of sparkling puddles, longer in the axis of the canyon, taking their ease in the shallow depressions aeons of wind had scoured out of the rocks. Water!

We ran forward, without a word, as though any sound might have sent them slithering away into the crevices beneath.

*Don't forget to measure them, depth as well*, we heard Ariella shouting in our phones as we leaned over the first one, our reflections quickly breaking up as twelve pairs of gloves scooped into the liquid and splashed it uselessly against our visors.

Szeto's glove came down at an angle and sent a thin sheet of the stuff all over Rodriguez. Rodriguez hit back and sent one over her. Others copied. Water dripped from our suits and ran off in little rivulets at our feet. Ariella's repeated pleas, exasperated rather than really cross, fell on deaf ears. Everyone was excited, elated, heady with the fun of it all after so many days cooped up in the rover. Then Lee picked up a flat slab of rock, perched himself above the puddle and dropped it right in. What water was left sprayed out all around, catching us at belt level.

And then, like breath on glass, the moist imprint of that lifeless little lake shrank rapidly to a last remaining patch of damp about a centimetre across, lingered for a few seconds more, and vanished. No rim of algae, no lichen, no change in rock texture at the water line, no twitching life-forms asphyxiating in a bed of sediment, signaled its fleeting visit. It was as though it had never existed. We moved on, took our measurements and samples, and fooled around a bit as well, but somehow the spontaneity of it all had evaporated, just like that water.

By the time we had finished there were just a handful of the deeper puddles left and we were ready for food. Breakfast seemed a long time back. You could eat in suit, not a meal of course, but a chew of dried bean curd or fruit (*marsbars* we called them) which a clip at chin level held within easy reach. It was easy to drop though, and once it had there was nothing you could do to retrieve it unless you stood on your hands and hoped it would drop back the way it had come. But then you had to somehow wedge it with your tongue or nose as you stood up to stop if dropping back again. You could drink as well, through a tube, but we hadn't brought anything with us for such a short outing. The emus the research teams used were much more sophisticated than the 1-hour outfits we had.

Which is why we were not equipped with an alarm relay from the base. It was only when we reached the lock and heard its attenuated screeching that we knew something was up. Lewis counted us, realised someone was missing, went back up the road and reappeared with Xing who, as usual had been looking under boulders for whatever he could find. (So far it had been an unusual trip, first a sleever - quite a big enough find for most of us - then a coin. A third find would have been unprecedented; the puddles didn't count; we'd pretty much been expecting them.)

Once inside, Lewis grabbed a handful of extra supplies while Ariella hurried us into the shelter. This was an L-shaped cavity down two flights of steps at the far end of the common area. We still had our suits on and it wasn't until Lewis had closed the half-metre thick hatch that we could get them off. The alarm had sounded just a few minutes after we had left but we were still okay. The warning from a still functioning planetary defense satellite told us that a proton shower from the Sun was hurtling towards us at 1.5 million kilometres an hour, slow enough to give us several hours of preparation time. But Lewis was taking no risks. Our suits would have protected us from the preliminary lighter bursts of radiation before the serious downpour blanketed the place, but you didn't mess with that stuff. Xing had been out the longest, but just a little over a minute and we didn't think any more of it. We were more concerned at how long we would be cooped up in the shelter. Solar storms could go on for days or be over in hours. Above us we had ten metres of rock and rego - our only protection in the absence of a protective layer of atmosphere.

*

The first few hours in the shelter - there was a nose-teasing ghost of an aroma in its still air - were fun; we ate some food, chatted a bit, sang a couple of songs and heard Lewis tell us about the time he had tasted meat - an incomer had given him a strip of biltong - and woken up full of remorse at what he had done, though he recognised that it was not he who had killed the beast in the first place and that not eating its flesh could have no retroactive effect.

Singer was clear on that point: sending your noodles back because they contained a bit of meat (we had none, by the way and still, mainly, do not) was not going to bring any animal back to life. The man was so unfanatical, so convincingly reasonable. We were all Singerites, if not by conviction at least by necessity, but most of us would have felt squeamish about eating animals had there been any to eat. We were not so odd in that respect, plenty here had felt the same, and despite the massive temptation and availability which did not exist out there.

We knew the history - the first ban, by one small country just before the millennium on all experiments involving primates. Creatures which exhibited the intelligence of bright toddlers and shared 98% of our DNA (shared 98% of *their* DNA with us) they had reasoned, could no longer be considered *lives unworthy of life;* could no longer be freely injected with toxins, strapped in cruel conditioning rigs, or slowly suffocated by pollutants, in the interests of human science. The new morality got a boost from other disturbing discoveries - and even more disturbing applications: that we could see through their eyes (alas, only literally) and that the big apes could be taught the rudiments of human language.

It had started with cats, an interface between feline brain and human technology - fuzzy pictures of a bearded face, and a woodland scene with forked branch in the foreground. Sticky ethical problems were quickly elbowed aside.

What if semi-articulate apes could be fitted with the device and trained to fire guns? No embarrassing body bags for chimps, no MIAs - and real-time video from yet another jungle theatre; perfect protection for the combat controllers safe in their filtered-air offices on the 145<sup>th</sup> floor, a continent away.

When the disk and transcripts of the first application, which was also the last, were leaked to the media, the artless expressions of pain and deception which the simple texts conveyed shocked the world's news consumers. For the first time they saw themselves as animals had always seen them. Even we felt the shame...

Charlie, big smiling Charlie at the plane place. Smiles at food; smiles at hug from controller; smiles at siblings. Ah! So cute! His picture is on. What we see now is through his eyes: close up of controller's ear, a checked shirt, a quick, panoramic view of plane place, then back to the controller's face, and then others, all with tight-fitting helmets that look as though they are sealed on. It's darker now - inside the plane. Switch off. Eight hours later, switch on again. Quick shot of ground - low hills, thick green; a brown path, oxbows on a river, sunlight on water, rising smoke, all coming much closer; long arms up cords, at least a hundred parachutes, floating down like dandelion seeds. Jumble, jumble, then picture steady again. They're on the bank. Oh God! What's that? Is he going to touch it? Round box with straight rods sticking out at angles. Closer. Two fingers of a hairy hand delicately move in to pick, a delicate, grooming movement. Screen goes blank. Screaming, ululation.

*Where Charlie? Where Charlie? Here Charlie leg. Where Charlie? Charlie not here. Where plane? Where Jim? Why Jim kill Charlie? I hear Jim voice. Jim not here. Where Jim?*

*Move forward. Forward good. Charlie naughty. Ernie is alpha. Next box nice. Move forward. See Jim at forward. All happy now. Move forward. Move forward.*

\*

Economics helped as well - feeding cattle had become prohibitively expensive, never mind the inefficiencies of meat-based feeding programmes to keep billions alive. Health issues also helped - few of us died of heart-related disease. Our diet was high in fibre. We ate like Incas, better in fact, and lived in the same thin air which floated around their mountain habitats. Quadrupeds were next - some nations less willing than others to forego centuries-old traditions, but driven to act by nightmarish diseases transmitted by beef cattle. I read with horror of old country practices - bears tapped alive for their bile - and the factory farms of the affluent West and Asia where the killing was done out of sight of the final consumers.

How will it be in the future? Will our future be the past again, irrigated by the blood of our not-quite kith and kin? Well, the killings have now stopped - the killings of those with the extra 2% (and the brains to kill each other), and those with 2% or more too few who were also their victims. Here we have few animals, apart from the bees. (A few months back we heard what we think was the bark of a dog, or maybe a deer, but nothing came of our searches. Strictly speaking there shouldn't be any larger mammals left.) I can't say it will never happen; we will not kill them of course, but elsewhere? We think there may be other pockets, and of course later, when the community grows and the memories of Settlement fade.

And when science begins again? And sacrifices? Ours is once more an elemental world. We understand it - the thunder, the changing faces of the moon, the darkening of the sun, the stab of lightning, the shaking earth - but those who do not? Superstition, religion - we watched in awe mingled with disdain (but that changed) their power over our two elderly neighbours when we first arrived. Yet how had they survived? Science tells us they should not have. Humanity will have to reinvent itself. I can only ensure that this small part of it starts off on the right foot. When we draw the face in the sand again, it must be a different face.

*

And then Ariella described the appendectomy she'd performed in the back of a rover in the middle of a dust storm. And time began to drag. At night - we just had the central screen to tell when that was - we lowered the lights and made ourselves as comfortable as we could on the brick beds. They reminded me of the *kang* my grandmother used to talk about, the heated platforms they slept on in the north of the old country. She'd read about them on the screen.

In the brickwork next to my bed someone had gouged a roundish pattern of lines, a bit angular and irregular in that gritty surface, but recognizable all the same. Underneath, barely decipherable, were the words:

*The path*
*The spider makes through the air*

*Invisible*
*Until the light touches it*

*The path*
*The light makes through the air*
*Invisible*
*Until it finds the spider's web*

And a name, Janet Lewis, perhaps the poet's - it didn't have a Settler ring to it. I was to check when I got back to Zube (and unearth her line: *the sunlight pours unshaken through the wind*, as reassuring then more than two centuries ago as it is now after so much has changed. It always comes back to me whenever I spend a quiet hour or two up on the hill, gazing out over the sunlit, empty ocean to our north or lie there on my back at night, telling the stars. Immune to flux, Orion, stark and spare, still shines forth. On his belt, Alnilam, Alnitak and Mintaka unrelentingly proclaim their dazzling alignment, as breathtaking to us as it was to the desert scientists who named them so long ago.)

We spread out the dried vetiver leaves a previous party had stacked in an alcove, but there were barely enough to go round. One, even two nights, would have been okay but a week there was something none of us wanted to even think about.

Was it the distinct smell of those leaves, a strange synergy of that, and the light and life those lines evoked? I don't know, but that night I dreamt of a great river which I followed from its beginnings high in mist-covered hills to the low-tide smell of its wide mouth. By lichen-covered rocks along the way I found a rabbit skull and in reeds by the water's edge the skeleton of a fish. Later, among seaweed, under a green-haired rock, I fished out the dark pink ball of a sea-urchin's shell. Behind me, the smooth surface of the tidal flats popped and bubbled; holes appeared, and little tailings, the work of invisible creatures blindly following their genes in the water-logged sand beneath.

*******

*One day when I was in my third year at school, Grandfather felt a severe pain in his stomach. Father tried everything he knew but it was no good. "The mind wants the medicine but the body rejects it", he said, half talking to himself. With all hope gone, he went off to order a coffin. When he returned he brought back with him the shavings of juniper for Grandfather to see.*

*The news spread quickly and everyone came to visit. There were relatives and clansmen from his old home, which was to be expected, but also friends and acquaintances from near and far, all with a gift for the dying man.*

*As the visitors left, Grandfather thanked them respectfully for their concern, wished them a long and happy life, and gave to each a silver dollar in memory of him.*

*On the evening of the sixth day his condition deteriorated rapidly. He was in great pain and I couldn't bear to watch. His bed was moved hurriedly to a room next to the main reception room in preparation for the worst. My two elder brothers sat in vigil as mother had just given birth and was in no condition to stay at her father's side. Father himself was terribly concerned. Unable to leave Grandfather for a moment in case he slipped away, he sent me off to buy more medicine in a last desperate attempt to save him.*

*The shop was two and a half kilometres away in the next village. In daytime there were even grown-ups who felt uneasy on the narrow path I had to take. And now it was night, but I didn't give a thought to the horrors I might meet on its remote and lonely stretches as I sped through the darkness. My only thought was for Grandfather and the medicine I had to buy for him. I arrived back home drenched in sweat.*

*When he had taken his medicine his spirits seemed to revive a little but there was no change in his general condition. Father had already bought a paper horse and carriage and placed them at Grandfather's bedside. They would carry his spirit to the Western Paradise. Two more days passed and then, at dusk on the second day, Grandfather set off on his final journey. I remembered the time we had gone to Fangliao, his home as a child. I was about eleven then. "You see the mountain behind where we live? It looks just like a carp coming out of the water, doesn't it?" he said to me between pulls on his pipe as we rested by a giant camphor log and breathed in its clean white tang. "You can build a house here and become a wealthy man, but if you want to become a great man you have to leave here, go abroad. Will you do that, Zhihong, when you grow up, go away and make a name for yourself out there?"*

I loved that passage as a child. (What *did* camphor smell like?) My grandmother frequently read The Fig Tree to me, peering closely at the screen from time to time when she couldn't remember the words. She was very old but the skin of her face was taut and smooth and honey coloured, with only the slightest wrinkling under her eyes. These were still Chinese in contour, like my own and my sister's, but where I have brown irises, hers were a pale jade. My sister has the same. We laughed about those things out there - we were such a cosmopolitan jumble of genes an anthropologist would have been hard put to classify us by our physical characteristics. Our family name was almost the only purchase (a string or two of language, a few poems, simple recipes, were others) we had on cultures long swamped by the oceans of time and space we had crossed.

It was funny, when you knew a person's name you could then perhaps detect a feature which hitherto you had considered as nothing more than a characteristic of that particular individual, and understand then why it was there. I've mentioned eyes, but there was hair, too, different colours of course, but different textures as well. Rodriguez, from his name, was American by ancestry - his hair sleek and dark above jet black eyes, full lips and a heavily bearded face; Xing, Chinese, but only his wispy beard and the barely detectable Asian-ness in his eyes correlated with his name. Zhudi was (still is) the same - fair-haired and green-eyed like Pei Yu, my sister, with a pale and fragile northern European skin (I'm much darker) so easily burnt by Earth's strong sun; only her eyes, and her name, give her distant ancestry away.

A name was an anchor holding us, just, to something back there which, even as the future Settlers had made their choice to leave, and we their descendants lived it, kept them, and us, from aimless drifting. Which is perhaps why we treasured it, as though aware that this one flimsy fluke was all that secured us to something beyond the immediate kinship we felt with our fellow Settlers, fulfilling a need for continuity, however unspoken. Maybe it was those concatenations of vowels and consonants, insubstantial though they were, mere puffs of breath: Han, Gutierrez, Ling, Ashrawi, Baalke, Kim, Mafala...which made it possible for us to start again on the other side of that terrible discontinuity which long before then the complex interactions of billions of gravitational fields, the gravity wells of stars bigger than a million Earth suns, of dumb, giant exo-planets, the pull of vast clouds of slowly tumbling rocks, and the faint but inexorable push of light, had contrived to blast between us and what had been.

*There is no such thing as a random event*, Shaw had told us in junior class. *Randomness does not exist - at least not in the context of the cosmos. Whatever is unpredictable is unpredictable because we don't have all the facts; nothing is inherently random, just random by default. Chaos* (here he would pause for effect; he loved the paradox of it all) *is ordered. No, I do not mean immutable, we're talking non-linear dynamics here - anything can happen en route (and that isn't random either). Laplacian determinism went out with Poincaré. A catastrophe* (the dinosaur killer, Chicxulub, was his favourite example*) is not random - it is the normal, repeat normal, behaviour of a chaotic system.*

The impactor was on its way, even then. Of course we didn't know that, but I liked Shaw's line. I didn't have much truck with the *in the Beginning was the Word*-stuff (however divine that old and elegant language). God, a Creator, might have existed; we didn't really care one way or the other. We were too modest, wary of the arrogance of those times when man believed, despite all the evidence to the contrary, that an alleged creator of all things, including a universe so old and vast that the light of its first spark took fourteen billion years to reach us, might possibly be interested in the transient bloom of babbling weeds dotting this *kongzhong zhi yi xiwu,* this speck of dust in the void, as the *Liezi* had called it, five hundred years before the Common Era.

I clung, still do, to a natural pantheism - the *Dao,* if you want. The ultimate beginning? The ultimate end? Metaphysics! The Dao does not speak of what it does not know. And anyway, even the Second Law of Thermodynamics precludes a pre-existing state of nothingness. The physical universe, Nature, grandmother told me, is *ziran*, that which is spontaneous, self-originating. It attributes nothing to a creator; it just is, in and of itself - a breathtaking inherence without why or wherefore, totally indifferent to our existence.

\*

Wu Zhuoliu's memoirs came back to me when we moved Grandfather; he weighed a little over 15 kilos, down here a human leaf. There was no juniper for the coffin, there was nowhere I could run to for medicine or help, and nowhere to buy the paper horse and cart. We didn't believe in all that stuff, but there was a dignity in death even there, which might surprise you after what I've just said.

From his bed we had laid him on the gurney. A square mat of woven leaves had been placed over it, overlapping on all sides, the corners to the top and bottom and to the sides. We placed his scrap of newsprint, the one with the clouds and raindrops and the names of cities, under his wispy beard. And when the Celebration had ended, we wrapped the mat round him, sides first, secured with a stalk rope, and then the top and bottom, creasing them inwards first before folding them down to meet each other. They were fastened in the same way. At that point my sister came forward with the dolly, a tightly patterned pad of dry stems through which fresh green stalks had been inserted and tied above it in a simple twist. As my mother and father lifted Grandfather up, one at his head, one at his feet, Pei Yu placed the dolly above the fastening, looped the two long strands which projected from it round the rustling package of grandfather's corpse, tied them together and then pushed the knot and loose ends tidily out of sight beneath her handiwork, for it was she who had woven it and shown to Grandfather while his eyes could still see.

*Wrapping zhongzi,* we jokingly called it. It was a bit like that, though wrapped corpses were never as tightly packed or full to bursting as those steaming leaf-bound bundles of dried fruit and grains which we helped Mama make from time to time. Death, even out there, was still death, and levity helped put it in its place, if the death were not amongst your own.

# The Return

I had been warned about it, or rather told it would happen. It wasn't dangerous, just so disconcerting. None of my companions seemed disturbed by what I was doing. I could hear Xing snoring fitfully, Zhudi stirring to a new position, the others as oblivious as they. And yet the travel and frequency of the reciprocation should have jerked them wide-eyed awake in seconds.

I was facing the exercise wall, my feet strapped in the immobilisers and my hands lightly gripping the two handles in front of me, pulling and pushing myself up to and away from the wall. Yet it was not I approaching the wall but the wall approaching me. I was fixed, or so it seemed, as immobile as my feet, while I brought the gray metal surface up to my nose and pushed it back again, tonnes of spacecraft at the tip of my fingers, sliding up to and away from me with the ease of a trolley on wheels.

I tried blinking, but this was no optical illusion, like that silhouette of a face which appears and disappears between two goblets as foreground and background vie for dominance. Off my downward-pulling world, away from its gravity, my brain was confused by the poverty of signals it was getting from the environment. Embedded in their gel, the tiny crystals of the otolith organs were, like everything else, weightless, dead to the acceleration they would have felt in gravity as my head moved forward to the wall; touch and pressure receptors in my feet and ankles no longer knew where down was; my limbs weighed

71

nothing; nothing told my brain where up was - there was no up, and the constant juggling of signal against signal in my muscles - relax, contract, relax again - to maintain my body's verticality and balance had ceased in the absence of sensory cues.

Strange that only when it is no longer there do we become conscious of gravity's all-pervasive and constant presence. We had left it behind us; we would experience it again, oppressively at first, when we reached our new and bigger home.

*How many you do?* I heard Xing sleepily ask me, snuffling away in that irritating way of his - a constant clearing and re-clearing of his airways which we all had to do (nothing drained away in zero gravity; phlegm just stayed there) but which he did more than the rest of us. We learnt why later.

*Twenty-five,* I replied, *then I stopped moving and the wall moved instead.*

I started again. Normality returned. Nostrils flaring, Xing was into a second round of snorting, shaking his head in frustration at the hopeiessness of his efforts. Zhudi, just awake, looked at me, her eyes - *Bear with it,* they said - holding mine a split second longer than a casual glance.

*Many more months of this,* I thought, *and even her tolerance will start fraying at the edges.*

Never in the history of humankind had so much been placed on eleven pairs of shoulders, a burden so paralyzingly momentous that it was only the tracassery of daily trivia that kept us sane...by threatening our sanity. An overflowing waste unit, a colleague's untidiness, Xing's nasal reveilles, an acrid armpit, and nowhere to go but the suffocatingly exiguous radiation shelter in the well of the craft, nine times out of ten already occupied by a fellow refugee from the hell that was other people. There was something masochistic about our mission; no-one had forced us to go. Carson's words came to mind - *in the long vistas of geologic time, man had no part...Despite our own utter dependence on this earth, this same earth and sea have no need of us.* So why bother?

We thought about it and didn't think about it - it was too huge to contemplate. Armageddon had come again, from space, from heaven. What arrogance made us think we could, should, reverse the process, transplant these frail, remaining strands of DNA and hope they would take root?

Officially, we were going to take a look; officially also, we knew we would not be going back. But Humanity II? We knew, and didn't want to know. W*ei wu* - rather than consciously will it or strive for it, let it happen, if nature so willed it...or not; the very idea of it crushed the breath out of you.

Was this Step 5 in the brief history of man, the final one before extinction, the end of our two seconds-worth of existence, which is all it amounted to - *tick-tock* - no more than that, if you compressed Earth's age to a single day? Step 1, off the trees into the grass; Step 2, out of Africa and Asia, to elsewhere, on foot; Step 3, out of elsewhere, by boat, across the oceans; Step 4, into a rocket, to the Moon, Mir, Mars, in the shallows of the Silver River, the Milky Way; three slippery stepping stones of trillions more, which we scrubbed dry, stabilized and perched upon, not sure where to go next. Or was it Step 1 again, mode 2? A jump back to Darwin's tangled bank, whatever was left of it, and a slow crawl forward again, simultaneously attracted and repelled by what we knew the future could hold?

\*

We had been gone a month and the "serious" traffic with Zube had long dwindled to a token exchange of phatic. Their signals took almost four minutes to reach us, ours four minutes to reach them. Anyway, what could they do but wish us well and ask after the equipment? The daily check-ins, even when communication had been instantaneous, quickly became nothing but a ritual, as both sides realized, reluctantly at first, a few days into the mission.

There was no going back. There was no chance of rescue should anything have gone wrong. That was soon brought home to us by the increasingly tenuous down-link to Mars, and our vain efforts (we had not really expected it to be otherwise) to acquire an up-link from Earth. Early on in the planning we had ruled out a free-return trajectory. This would have brought us back to our starting point if the propulsion unit had failed, or we screwed up aero-breaking at the Earth end of the journey. But time was a factor: a trade-off had to be made between the psychological reassurance free return provided - *if you don't get there, you come straight back, well, sort of* - and life support reliability, which would have had to be guaranteed for another year and a half at least for the slower Mars-bound leg of an aborted mission. Anyway, what good was psychological reassurance if the return trip itself was a test of sanity few would pass?

We knew about Apollo 13, more than two centuries ago - a free return had saved them, but their total mission time to the Moon and back was less than week. As it was, a minimum energy Hohmann transfer (which paradoxically required us to leave Mars when Earth was at its farthest from us on the other side of the sun) plus some extra propellant, had brought our transit time down to a little over 270 days without compromising the mass ratio. That allowed us to exploit the craft's double and triple redundancy in the mission-critical systems, retrofitting even more to be on the safe side, and carry the stores we needed, both for the trip itself and at mission's end. We had little idea what we would find, apart from a still breathable atmosphere. We were, we felt, as safe as we could be in that hostile environment, but well and truly alone despite the well-intentioned attempts of the Settlement to keep our spirits up.

*Knock!......Knock!..................................*
*.................Who's*
*there?..........................................Zube.........*
*.......................................Zube*
*who?.................................................Zu*
*berior beings from the Planet Mars!*

Yes, we liked it, we told them (already *they* were *them*), send us more. But as five minutes grew to ten and ten to fifteen and the round trip light time stretched what, closer in, would have been ten seconds of tolerable banter into a numbing thirty minutes, we talked less and less. In a few months, Earth, blithely spinning larger and larger, as if nothing had happened, would be just seconds of light time away and getting closer all the time.

Eleven people in 60sq. metres of living space, small even by Settlement standards, made us appreciate what we had back there. It was designed for eight but we were eleven - we needed the expertise of hunter-gatherers and survivalists, not paleo-hydrologists or isotope geologists. And we needed couples who could breed, though re-population was not our stated aim. In any case at that stage we did not know, and even now that we are here still do not know, what the toll was. Communication had ceased overnight, which meant the big centres had certainly gone, but new centres could have been set up if enough had survived. But we had heard nothing in the thirty-five years since it happened and have heard nothing since our arrival.

But it was hard to believe nothing had survived, that somewhere in that corrosive darkness and cold of the first two years, pulses had not continued beating in their fleshy propagules deep in some cave or tunnel, in a submarine perhaps, or ocean vent research vessel, or in some high mountain valley, a Shangri-la saved from destruction by...what? Again hard to imagine. We'd done impacts at school and again in post-qual; they were unforgiving. And a triple one - two oceanic, one terrestrial - was the worst possible scenario. Jupiter had absorbed the twenty-one lumps of Shoemaker-Levi with all the aplomb of a cloud raked by gunfire. But two fragments of a contact binary, a giant rock peanut, nine kilometres by five, and its faithful satellite, impacting at 40,000kph at ten-minute intervals on rock-solid, iron-cored Earth? The biosphere, Man, and all his works had been wiped off its surface, or at least so we had to suppose, though we knew it had happened many times before, long, long before we had made our appearance. But there was no mistaking the change in colour of the once blue planet as we observed its darkened disk across 300 million kilometres of space, in those early post-impact years.

And then there was the silence; the drizzle of voice mail from Earth, the bips and beeps of compressed data, the monitors droning away - all that went, not instantaneously, like someone throwing a switch, but raggedly, as though some giant hand had slowly rent in two the electro-magnetic fabric between us, until only a few strands were left, and then snapped them as well. And then, behind the trails of millions of radio and television transmissions which since Marconi onwards had propagated their way two hundred light years into space, past the Moon, past the Sun, past the dour, dark mass of Planet X on its plodding six-million-year orbit of the same sun, by then a faint star five thousand billion kilometres away, past Alpha Centauri, past Epsilon Eridanus and ever onwards, never to stop, never to catch up with the ever expanding universe, a radio void, radio death, nothing. The electronic yawp had ceased; Earth had closed down.

*

The hab was basically a cylinder divided into three sections joined by a central shaft, or tunnel, depending on whether you felt vertical or horizontal. Right at the bottom, or top, or right at one end, whatever, lay the orange wall of the storm shelter-cum-cargo hold. Orientation, you have to realize, was a complex issue - there was no absolute verticality which the unfailing presence of gravity would have provided.

Yet even in the lack of it, ingrained habits were hard to ignore. Top was still where the ceiling was, bottom the floor, and when we talked to each other for any length of time, we unfailingly aligned ourselves with those comforting points of reference. Some were more resistant than others: two or three bodies blocking access to a shaft into the next level should not have been a problem; we were as little constrained as fish in water or birds in the air - anyone wishing to get in had only to use the space between the top of their heads and the ceiling or between the soles of their feet and the floor. Not Mafala - she would wait till they moved.

Left, right, up, down - to ignore them was to enter an unsettling world of unfamiliar perspectives and spaces. It was like standing on your head with your feet against the wall in a room you thought you knew intimately. Where was that cracked brick? The shirt you had kicked across the floor? Or flashing the light on and off in a room you had never entered. An impression of strangeness. Volumes you had never imagined filled voids you had never suspected were there; expectancy was thwarted in a surreal reconfiguration of a reality you had never sought to question. There was no one definable space, but spaces, potentially as many as there were positions to view then from.

And that was not all; I had been looking through the observation port at the still dimly visible contours of the Settlement. Imagine the cross-wires of a targetting device - I was the vertical line and, as it happened, aligned head and toe with the longitudinal axis of our craft; the Settlement, as I viewed it, lay along the horizontal axis. I watched it slowly disappearing as the reddish disk turned on its axis. I turned from the port to reply to some remark Zhudi had made and in that instant, verticality went and I was…horizontal, lying along the axis as if on an invisible cot. Nothing had changed - my feet were still anchored, my hands on the port - only my head had moved.

Sometimes it was even more alarming - one second you were vertical in one direction and then the next you were, or felt you were, standing on your head, flipped through 180 degrees, without moving a muscle, and again that strange feeling of seeing things as though you really were upside down, but that somehow your eyes were in you toes. Or you looked left and your body slid off right, as though detached from your head.

*

We all had our own lair of relative privacy - a cramped cachot, which weightlessness made easier to bear, with sleep harness and restraining strap for your head, which otherwise would have floated off the pillow, locker, water squirt, screen, and liquid waste facility (solid was handled by a central processor in the storage area), and no porthole. To see further than 12 metres you had to go to a common area on level 2 where, apart from the monitors fore and aft, a small transparent rectangle about 15cm by 25cm was our only eyeball on the outside.

In the first few days we had spent a lot of our time almost queuing up for a look, a last look, at our home. Hands clamped on either side of our face to cut out the cabin light (the very same gesture I saw in the lake couple a few days after we landed), we watched as its features slowly faded: the poles, Olympus Mons, the volcanoes of Tharsis - three vicious boils on the face of a small giant - and the ragged gash of the Valley where, years ago, I had made up my mind to leave, and that Zhudi would be with me, without knowing quite how it was all going to come about.

Then interest fell off and we entered the quiescent phase after the adrenalin-driven high of departure, as the literature had said we would: a lot of reading, listening to music, diary writing, and long, revealing talks one on one with fellow crew, whom we got to know for the very first time, though we had been friends or acquaintances for years.

\*

Towards the end of the second month it became obvious to us that Xing's snuffling was more than the usual nasal congestion. He had bad headaches and I was alarmed to discover, as I palped him one day at his request to confirm his own findings, that there were swellings at the side of his neck. We had no doctor as such on board but three of us had some medical expertise and, more importantly, access to diagnostic and how-to software. Doctors were generally considered bad for crew morale, so dispersing some of their expertise around without designating anyone in particular as the doc was a well-tested solution.

We hadn't ruled out illness on board; most of us had thrown up liberally in the first few days of weightlessness and experienced spells of debilitating vertigo and the usual snuffles and sore throats and ears for at least a couple of weeks thereafter, but we knew about that and just waited for it to pass, which it did.

Grazed heads and bruised backs were another problem in the first few days, as we rammed torpedo-like into whatever we had been heading for; until we learnt to push off with just the right amount of force and float to a gentle stop at our destination.

We were worried by things like ruptured appendices, or choking or toothache and had gone through the protocols several times before departure. We suffered very little from the contagious diseases common on Earth - no measles (just one outbreak in a hundred years, brought in by an incomer) or dysentery or cholera - and rarely from genetic disorders, which had already been largely eliminated by the end of the 21$^{st}$ century as the human genome shed its secrets.

So when all the indications suggested that Xing was suffering from naso-pharyngeal cancer, we were devastated. We couldn't cut it out, we couldn't radiate it, we had no chemotherapy, and no hope of help when we arrived. Pre-departure checks had revealed nothing untoward. I immediately thought of that incident in the Valley. Had he over-remmed in those few minutes longer he had stayed outside than the rest of us? He might have, but then leukemia would have been a more likely outcome, not that there was anything we could have done about that either. So we ruled that out as cause. But at least, we thought, allocating a cause might help us to deal with the problem psychologically.

Xing was already ahead of us. Despite his northern name and a gene pool fed by generations of currents from other communities, a recurrent feature of his ancestral DNA, he told us, was southern Chinese, diluted, attenuated in some generations, thicker in others, but potentially the mystery vector which had finally delivered that death sentence. For it was among southern Chinese that naso-pharyngeal cancer (he knew the name for it in Cantonese) had struck the most. It gnawed away at the very centre of a person's sense of identity.

There had been extensive screening, but not everyone wanted it (just because the gene was there didn't mean it would express itself) and not everyone got it, and there had been errors. Anyway, the gene had got as far as Xing with no adverse effect. But then, some minute change, perhaps indeed a winging blow from a stray proton, a barely perceptible nudge from the proverbial anemone's tentacle, had roused it from its long hibernation at the bottom of the gene pool and sent it bobbing to the surface and a short life of mayhem and destruction, just like the impactor.

The prognosis was poor; death was a few months away, even perhaps before we arrived. And we were no longer at Zube, where a digester was close by. We didn't like to think about that; there was no hatch we could use, except the one we would blow on landing. There would be no burial in space: a puff of air, then a slowly tumbling shape growing smaller and smaller till it disappeared from view, perhaps only to be seen again, if the trajectory were right, by a curious child watching the heavens on some quiet prairie *Look, Mom, a shooting star - wheeeeee!* as it burnt up in the upper air.

We were going to be together, all the way there, all the way down. Unpleasant calculations filled our minds. If he died soon what would we do? In the more than 200-year history of long-distance space travel no one, miraculously, had died en route with months to go before arrival. The few deaths there had been had occurred just days before arrival. The statistics even talked about MEDs, *mission-end deaths* - a suspected over-preparation for landing in the body's psycho-physiological response to the torpor induced by months in zero gravity and isolation, whatever the regimes devised to prevent it.

There had been deaths in low-orbit space stations, even a handful of this-universe-isn't-big-enough-for-both-of-us homicides, but space stations were basically a suite of rooms with several doors into a refrigerator, space itself. A protected corpse could be moored at the door for easy retrieval at the next docking. But that was not for us, and we had no emus either, a risk we had taken voluntarily, confident in the integrity of our life-support system and nuclear engines. One could have been used as a makeshift body-bag, but after more than a few days decomposition gases would have turned it into a time bomb. We had considered the possibility of siphoning off a couple of litres at a time but our airscrubbers were for gently suffocating $CO_2$, not toxic gases. The health hazard of droplets of decomposition liquids floating around in our air supply was another matter.

The other solution - we hated ourselves for even considering it while he was still there before us - was Xing's own idea; he knew all too well what problems his dead body would cause.

Everyone had come to Level 2, their desire to reassure Xing coexisting awkwardly with the sure knowledge that he knew what they knew and nothing they said could change it. Only he could put us at our ease, which he did.

*Cut me up. Use the manual, it's all in there. Small enough to go in the waste disposer, so no more than 15 by 15 by 10, if you can do that neatly. It'll be messy but less so if you let rigor set in first. You'll have to smash my skull. Ling can do that – okay Ling?*

Visions of a Tibetan sky burial filled my mind - viscera coiled over rocks; marrow seeping from shattered bone; a crushed skull; the macabre ballet of the eviscerator, the circling vultures. Ling didn't let the tone drop.

*It'll be my pleasure. This hammer do?*

Jagged banter was the norm between them but it was Xing who had once saved Ling's life - he had choked on some badly husked fonio and it was Xing who had sliced into the membrane between the thyroid and cricoid cartilages to get him breathing again, knowing that if he had sliced through his vocal nerves he might never have spoken again.

*

But that was all in the future. We still had Xing, alive, and as impulsive as ever. We would take it as it came; we were not short of painkillers - and for head pain they worked even better in zero G. He had all the psychological support he needed, twenty-four hours a day, and his own resilient self.

He still helped me with my oulips, with just the minimum of condescension to be expected of an amateur expert in hypergraph theory and combinatorics (Graeco-Latin bi-squares were his speciality). I was, to put it mildly, more on the verbal side. But like many Settlers before us, inured to the austerity of life under plastic, we both recognised in the self-imposed constraints of the oulip an analog of our own condition - restricted, bound, hedged about with don'ts, it was that sparsity of choice in our lives which made whatever we could create so valuable, just as from those enclosing lattices there emerged distillations of great inventiveness and beauty which one could never have predicted from the initial lousy deal.

> *in the pool*
> *look!*
> *the cool moon...*
> *food for my mood*

I remember writing that, a constraint so light that Xing dismissed it out of hand - *yeh yeh, words with double o's* - and told me to try something with a lambda x-matrix instead. But I was happy with my little haikoid and the twin moonlets of each word which in their evocation of what was still before us maintained a link with what we had left behind. Can any one imagine the intensity of my hankering for a landscape bathed in that light? I had read and loved Whitman:

> *Smile, O voluptuous cool-breathed Earth!*
> *Earth of the slumbering and liquid trees!*
> *Earth of the vitreous pour of the full moon.*

The vitreous pour of the moon! I shivered with pleasure at the thought of it. No such magic slip had ever spilled from our two dusty potatoes to transform the arid features of Mars.

*

In the months after Xing's condition was revealed I spent more time in meditation. Weightlessness removed so much sensory input that entering the state was much easier; here I have to push against a swarm of intruding reminders. Out there we all practised it; it was a recognised therapy for the two extremes of long-duration space flight, boredom and stress. As deputy mission leader, the times became ever more frequent when I felt an almost overwhelming urge to be anywhere but there. Sleep was one way out, but one never woke up with that (what I would call now *rain-washed*) clarity of vision peculiar to the emergence from a meditative trance.

Each sleeping space had its yantra. My own was a schematic projection of Earth, Africa to the fore, surrounded by the curving lines, visible and invisible, of the magnetosphere. There was nothing magic or sacred about the diagram, just a simple design painted on the panel opposite the sleep harness. (Zhudi's was the spiral structure of a seashell.) I would harness up, focus on the yantra, and then, like an unobserved particle, I was not there - or rather everywhere and nowhere and aware of neither, a void in a void, out of existence, out of time, a mere potential, unrealized, unrealizing, an unexpressed inherence...until something, I never knew what, a random firing of a neurone, a fluctuation in the ambient temperature, some stray noise - a fart, a belch, an ecstatic groan - ruptured the seamless sphere of my non-being and, like the particle from its collapsing wave function, I popped into existence again.

At night, i.e. the time we switched off the main lights and retreated to our rest space, the silence was complete, save for the diffuse whisper of the air exchanger. (Sometimes, suddenly awake, we lost it and listened in panic for our ear to pick up its edgeless murmuring again). No sound from outside, no creaks or pings of flexing metal. The odd yawn or snuffle from a neighbouring space, a burst of muffled words as someone talked in their sleep, served only to reinforce the totality of our isolation and that unsettling feeling that rather than hurtling through interplanetary space - there was no sense of forward movement - we were simply waiting there for something to end. And at the side of our heads, always, the silent but persistent caress from the sleep-safe vent, gently pushing away the suffocating cloud of $CO_2$ which, left to itself, would have built up around us as we exhaled.

But I enjoyed the act of going to sleep. Strange things happened behind your eyelids - exploding streaks and balls of light lit up the inner darkness as particles from the ends of the universe zipped through our craft and us as though we weren't there. Stranger still was the so called Lebedev effect they produced - an intense re-imaging of whatever had been the last thing you looked at, or even envisaged in your mind's eye, before closing your eyes. It was like a hologram, brightly lit and knife-edge sharp in startling 3-D.

\*

I had been counting the days, as had Zhudi. I hadn't spoken to the others about it - I didn't need to -

but knew that Zhudi and the other women had spoken together and that they and their partners were also counting. We'd talked about it, sporadically, long before we left, before any decision had been made to attempt a return to what was still then a damaged and darkened planet. But the discussions had been academic, a "what if" scenario none of us had suspected we would be part of.

Then, as plans crystallized, and faces we knew or came to know, replaced numbers, and the full import of what we might achieve came home to us, it was never far from our minds.

It was not going to be a first; there had been a handful of children. No, that's misleadingly imprecise: there were five of them and everyone, even us, knew who they were or had been. The first was Hubernik, Indian mother, American father, conceived, but not planned, on Pegasus-2 in 2021, on the way back from an early expedition - and all of them objects of an all-pervasive curiosity for science and the media alike. What was new were the circumstances, which might have turned that private act into a private ceremony of immense and overwhelming significance but which, in the event, didn't.

We had made love five or six times since our departure, not a lot. Like the other women's, Zhudi's cycle was still in pharmaceutical hibernation. We knew the rough limits; we had not bought kits with us which would have told us immediately; weight was at a premium and we knew that eventually the cycle would start again and we could just calculate for ourselves when the best time was.

Yes, in the background we were aware that that might be it, but it was hard to see in our self-absorbed coupling the genesis of Humanity II. More up close and personal, the enhanced sense of pleasure and oneness sex in zero gravity created quickly pushed aside any sense of momentousness, any awareness of possible outcomes. Eyes closed, I had effectively disappeared. No signals told me where my body was. I was a hub of pleasure, the white hot core of a sphere. Zhudi told me later she felt the same. It was as though we had imploded to a point of maximum density; we were the other side of the event horizon from which nothing escaped. The peripheral no longer existed. We were the wave front of a million tsunamis all hurtling towards the same point - inward, inward, inward.

Without opening my eyes, I flexed my fingers and wriggled my toes - my arms and legs relocated themselves; I could feel Zhudi doing the same. We drifted between the panels, fending off with elbows or feet. Our embrace had not slackened but we were no longer one - our star had collapsed; we were fragments again. I pulled Zhudi round to face in the right direction, placed my hands on her shoulders, kissed her and then, with a gentle push, launched her softly feet-first towards her cubicle.

*Watch your head,* I said, as I pushed off from the side to enter my own.

The others could come out - our Personal Hour, as the euphemism had it, was over.

That was Day 46 of the seventh month, S177...or 2206.

It struck me then, whether that was a significant birthday or not (as it happens, it wasn't - our first child was conceived about three weeks later, three weeks closer to Earth) that our old calendar would immediately lose its raison d'être once we had arrived. We would swap a great elliptical orbit round the sun for a tightly circular one; a year of 669 days for a year of 365. And instead of twelve long months ranging in length from 46 days to 65 we would have twelve short ones of almost equal length.

\*

Did they know we were there? What we were doing? Where we were going? Was someone watching us? Asking the same questions? They were not alone, we knew that - we were there; who else changed their water or took their honey? But that was from our perspective. Nothing could have persuaded us that we were being watched or that the hits had been deliberate, an act of barbarism on a cosmic scale. And yet such questions did seep into your consciousness as you watched them about their business. And all of us spent long hours watching them - at times just a seething mass, a super-organism, twitching and fluttering as one, at others, fragments no longer fragments but a whole in their own right, as singular as that very first bee above the clover strip, in clumsy swoops and feints struggling for a wing-hold in that strange air which separated one side of their plastic hive from the other.

Once, one escaped. We watched it try to fly, unguided by the scent of distant flowers or the dance of other bees, a bee lost in space, pushed by the blast from the mixer which, in the absence of convection currents, kept our air moving. From surface after surface it tried to launch itself back into this spare medium, its senses grappling for a clue, a stray molecule of nectar, a whiff of pollen, a reason for its helplessness, until, visibly exhausted, it aroused our pity and let itself be transported back to the hive between a pair of chopsticks.

How special those bees were! Genetically modified, they lived longer - at least a year, much longer than their ancestors, but it wasn't that which made them special; it was their mere existence. For apart from them and the swarms in the Settlement, there were no bees anymore...anywhere. The tiny tracheal mite, the barely bigger varroa, and the killing cold of half-empty hives unable to keep their falling populations warm by weight of numbers in the winters of post-millennium Earth, had silenced the buzzing for good.

Pollen and nectar remained where they were, unvisited. Feral swarms had disappeared completely by 2100; all domestic colonies by 2150. Lab bees were all that was left. In the US an annual forty billion dollars dropped out of the economy; in Europe, sixty-five billion. Alfalfa, melons, oranges, pears, apples, berries of all kinds, cucumbers, broccoli, beans, sunflowers, clover, squash, almonds ...over a hundred crops had waited in vain for the pollinator. Fire-blight and gray mould flourished, unchecked by the bacillus spores that bees commandeered by scientists had started delivering to their plants as chemical controls failed. Attempts to use the pollen beetle had come to nothing. Of the 30,000 known species of bee, not one survived, along with tens of thousands more not yet identified. Consumption of junk food soared as all but the most affluent consumers shunned vegetables, fruit and nuts. Then junk food itself went up, and with it dairy products - cheese, milk, butter, yoghurt - as cattle food, especially alfalfa, grew scarcer and scarcer. Shortages, rationing, malnutrition, starvation - for the post-industrial economies these hitherto insignificant spectres on the distant horizon, the insubstantial bogeymen of doomsters and bee freaks, lurched menacingly one giant step nearer to their world.

In desperation, governments turned to the seas. *Markelsization* was the watchword - a process and a philosophy: fertilize the sea - that was the process; privatise the harvesting - that was the philosophy. After all, it had worked on land; what was so sacrosanct about the sea that millions of square kilometres couldn't be farmed by private companies? Anyway, if the world wanted fed, the notion that the sea was a publicly held commons would have to go. The Moon or Mars weren't exactly flowing with milk and honey, so whatever size the world population reached, the larder was Earth and nowhere else.

Back in the pre-millennium, Markels himself had leased 2.7 million square kilometres of the Pacific from a drowning island microstate, poured in fertilizer...and almost overnight created a plankton bloom large enough to be seen from space. It worked. Where ten pounds of feed had produced a measly one pound of beef, one pound of fertiliser produced 4000 pounds of plankton. No-one human wanted to eat plankton, but they didn't have to. That was bottom of the food chain stuff. It was the top of it which liked the glop, and how! Five hundred tonnes of harvestable fish per square mile for a yearly dose of 5 tonnes of fertiliser...

We didn't know then how the seas would be, and we still don't know, only that there is now a lot less land and they are a lot warmer. We are on a coast. One day someone will find out, not us perhaps, but those who come after us, if any come. There are eight children now, three more on the way. The future seems a very long way ahead. I sometimes wonder if it's there at all. Maybe this is it. Rather than the beginning, perhaps we are the end.

*

Last night we lay on our backs by the lake - Zhudi, myself and the two children. They are slowly becoming aware, especially the elder one, of who we are.

*Dad, did you really come from up there?*

Up there, Mars flickered redly against a chattering backdrop of stars. We had been watching Spica coming nearer and nearer till the gap between them was barely a thumb-width wide. But it was not to be - just a trick of perspective. They were drawing apart again and the entanglement was over.

And on *Huo Xing,* the Fire Planet, on that cold and unclothed world where fire could not breathe, were they watching us? They knew we had made it, but nothing else. We could send no more signals, not even giant smoke rings or reflections from giant mirrors, and even if we could do, they would see nothing at that distance, not even with the most powerful telescopes in the world.

We swam in the lake. I told them what I did up there, and they would try to do the same, splashing heavily back before they were even half-way out.

*Draw a dolphin, Dad!*

I told them I had never seen a real one but they still wanted to know. And I showed them our cube dances (how clumsy I had become!). They practiced jackhammers and windmills as best they could and gasped in amazement when I told them that three backflips was normal for suicides.

*Without touching the ground once?*

*Not once!*

For in that gentler pull we flared with the speed of circular saw blades and flipped high into the air like the skittles of the world's finest jugglers.

*

We have no screens here, or rather the dozen or so we had on board had ceased to work shortly after we arrived. Maybe it was the landing or something corrosive in the air we can't detect, whatever - anyway, they don't work. So I and the other adults are their only source of knowledge. And I am aware that with us memory stops, knowledge stops, and they will be on their own, no more able to explain or replicate the commonplace technologies they know from us than the time-travelling youngster in the sci-fi story can explain to the alchemists the glowing green face on his wrist. Or why his cell phone - *Ah! You speak to people who are not here?* - works with waves. *Waves? In the air? Which you can't see?*

*What was it like driving a rover?*

*Why couldn't you go outside?*

*Can we go there?*
*Did you really run everywhere?*

Concentric ripples propagated across the taut surface of the lake towards the bank; closer by, a small something plopped into its warm, stilly waters; moonlight glinted off a pair of dark wings. A bat? A bird? A moth? And over it all, as soft as cloud shadow, a faint scent drifted down on us from the moist night air. I even thought I could taste a sweetness on my lips. Could they understand?

Only once up there, outside the Settlement, did I ever experience that sense of one-ness with the landscape, a feeling of melting into it, of being absorbed by it, to the extent that "I" was willingly suffused with a sense of something greater than self, a perfect congruence of observer and observed. Here it happens all the time (*Dad's off again,* I faintly hear them saying) but then I am predisposed, by virtue of my short life-time ever behind visors and pressure suits, to experience it more than your ordinary human animal. And while the process here is a gentle one, up there, that one time, it was less a melting, a mutual relaxation of one into the other, than a sudden and violent fusion.

We had been shooting cores on a field of evaporites when the storm hit. For thirty-six hours it raged around us and when we finally emerged into the ruddy gloom the low-lying landscape of small rocks and outcrops had changed beyond recognition. In its place, for as far as the eye could discern through the dim light, stood giant dunes, aligned east-west, like stranded pods of monstrous whales washed up on some alien beach.

Grainfall was still occurring, a fine dry rain of particles which the winds had harried thousands of metres into the air. And as these sifted down, a great fugue of primal groans, half sound, half sensation, exploded raggedly out of the piled-up sand and rolled over us, through us, underneath us, sweeping us up in its dark, churning turbulence, like boulders in a torrent.

I had a sensation of mighty beasts blindly stampeding through me, trumpeting their fear as they hammered the ground with their massive hooves. I had no sense of standing or lying or struggling for balance; I was the vibration, the noise, cresting and troughing with the waves, rising and falling in phase with them. And then I could feel the ground again and hear my companions telling me something. Slowly the fugue stopped, to be replaced by dispersed hummings and boomings, some less than a second in length, others much longer.

They pointed towards the nearest dune. I looked, and as I did so, a low, throbbing drone shot from its leeward slope as the accumulating sand, tipped past its angle of repose by the continuous shower of particles, cascaded down to the desert floor. More avalanches followed, all accompanied by the same innard-pummeling boom, even in that thin air, as dune after dune shed its excess load.

There are no dunes here, but I had read tales of this phenomenon before. Marco Polo mentions them, Darwin mentions them, and Chinese and Arabic texts going back a thousand years speak in awe of their eerie, sound-emitting properties, the ghostly sounds of invisible armies and evil desert spirits. Near Dun Huang, there are dunes which boom and shudder.

*

The children love hearing about life up there.
*Were there really two moons?*
*Tell us about the sleever again. Were you scared?*
*Have you still got that metal thing you found? Can we see it?*
They bounce around with the spring of rubber balls; I felt water-logged when I first arrived and the draining process has been slow. There is still a heaviness but I've adapted, like the others, and so far there have been no signs of strain, but I know that one day something might give.

We've no God-given claim to this place but that pull is persuasive in a way that only I and the others can experience. I yield to it, as I know we must yield in other things. *Rang,* says the Dao, "yield", and I do. They tried possessiveness, and were rapidly losing what they thought was theirs when the impactor hit. Even if it had missed they would have had no more than a few more decades before such a swift and final end might almost have seemed a welcome solution to their disintegrating world. (Hawking's estimate of another thousand years had been too optimistic by far.) But now we (*they* have gone) know that non possessiveness is our only hope. The arrogant teleology which said that this had been been made for us has had its day. Old Bao's precocious 12-year old said it all in the *Liezi*, 2600 years ago:

*It is only by reason of size, strength or cunning that one particular species gains mastery over another, or that one feeds upon another. Man catches and eats those that are fit for his food, but has heaven produced them just for him? After all, mosquitoes and gnats suck his blood and tigers and wolves devour his flesh, but does that mean he was made for them? There are ten thousand creatures in the universe, all the living things, and in this category there is nothing noble and nothing mean.*

Man, humanity, can no longer be the measure of all things. Humanity! You see how the arrogance remains - that's us: ten adults, eight children, three more on the way, and the lake couple we have found here! Is that an MVP? A Minimum Viable Population?

Now you see what I meant when I talked about species-awareness in my opening lines. The irony is that in one sense we're the saviours, one tiny sub-population - the Settlers - of another sub-population, the eleven billion people on Earth which (our two miracle survivors apart) no longer exists. We were a distant part of the boom, a 3000-strong fraction of the human meta-population. Without us, humanity would now be extinct; just another species of the millions before it which have disappeared for ever. We left our own isolated habitat island, "migrated" here, recolonised their habitat and re-established the species. But in another sense, the roles have been reversed - from source population, a breath of new life, we have become a sink population. The two-second boom is over - perhaps we are now already in the crash part of that explosive growth. If we don't make it, the only source which can save us is 400 million miles away. I doubt it will happen twice.

We're tottering on the edge of extinction, just like hamsters were over two centuries ago, but with one big difference - no one's going to help us out of our bottleneck. And what's worse, we know we're in one.

Hamsterman! How are the mighty fallen! A viability analysis of our little tribe would tell us that for mammals like us fifty is the barest minimum for survival. Less than that (though our diversity will help us some) inbreeding takes its toll - sperm abnormalities, weakened immune systems, compromised brain function. So we might survive, but dumber, less resistant, flawed - modern-day Neanderthals. Yet better off than them in one respect: we won't have ourselves to compete against.

Optimism without hope? I can live with it. Beneath this sheltering sky what more does one need?

\*

On Level 2 light floods into the ship from the port; a torrent of photons pours mercilessly onto the gaunt, grey face of Xing, the skin sucked in tight between the jaw and cheek bones as if inside there's a vacuum. When we roll the hab he can see Earth; he spends a lot of time looking out now. His breathing is fast. He is in great distress, even with the drugs. He eats little; swallowing is difficult. We can't rig up a drip, fluids don't drip in zero G, and when we try to inject under pressure he bruises so badly he asks us to stop. We are nearly there, just a couple of weeks out. Zhudi sits with him - she holds his hand against her belly; he closes his eyes. Zhuangzi, yes, Zhuangzi, what did he say? He feels the kicks, the start of a cycle he is soon to complete. Inside his head he speaks through his hand to himself in the womb:

*Life is the follower of death, and death the predecessor of life. Since death and life thus attend upon each other, why should I account either an evil?*

*Death, fetid and putrid, is deemed hateful, but the fetid and the putrid, returning, is transformed again into the spirit-like and wonderful. Therefore is it said, in the universe there is but one qi.*

*We are one, little one*, he tells himself; *I live on through you;* and feels a bit better. *Ji - san - ji - san -* accumulation, dispersion, accumulation, dispersion, on and on without extinction the *qi* remains, the eternal float.

Maybe that was wrong, my macabre vision of Xing eviscerated, eaten by vultures - too human, too man-centered.

*To share those wings and those eyes -*

*What a sublime end of one's body, what an enskyment; what a life after death.*

This from Jeffers' Vulture, half a century before the millennium, which I had read avidly in my late teens.

And from Lew Welch, a few years later, the same relaxed perspective, the bird of death as bird of re-birth and continuance:

*Buzzard meat is rotten meat made sweet again.*

But it was difficult for me, then, and still is, to make that conceptual leap, to separate death from extinction, cause from effect, to feel instead the whole resonating as one, a mutual interdependence in which linearity disappears. He knew I would have none of it; my grandmother had seen to that: *the sharpness of the knife disappears when the blade breaks* she told me more than once. She devoured the sceptics - Wang Chong, Fan Chen, Liu Qi, Huan Tan and the many others - and made sure I knew about them too.

What was that story? The one about the forest fire racing up to the town and the prefect, Liu Kun, who begs for the wind to change? The wind changes direction. Then in another town there are tigers, dozens of them, snatching babies from their hammocks and dragging the aged from their pallets. Liu arrives and what happens? The tigers jump into the Yellow River with their cubs on their back and are never seen again.

*How did you do it?* asks the Emperor, amazed at his powers.

*Ou ran,* Liu replies. Just pure chance.

*Truly a superior man,* says the emperor, as the court sycophants, nonplussed by his reaction, quickly rearrange their expressions and stop sniggering.

But then I wasn't dying, Xing would say. Zhudi holds him, knows our baby calms him, despite his despair, knows the memories we will have when he is gone help him face what is coming.

*One breath of Earth; get me down alive, then I'll go,* he laughs.

*Tell your baby about me, Zhudi.*

I used to tell him that the only *qi* he would be getting near to was the *qi* in *zhao qi,* the methane in our first Earth-made digester. But that was before. By that time spiky banter was out, unless he initiated it, which he did on his good days. But I was glad that the baby gave him some comfort and if some of the ancients gave him similar comfort I was not going to weigh in with counter-arguments from others among them, whatever strength they gave me.

The others sat with him as well; there was no roster, it wasn't a duty we felt obliged to perform; even in near-death he exerted a charm few could resist.

*

We knew our noises - human ones, equipment ones; you had to. No noise could be ignored until we knew what it was, where it was coming from. But after eight and a half months I could have inventoried all of them. We knew there was one we hadn't yet heard, but as we didn't really think we would be hearing it, given the odds, we sort of put it out of our minds. It was, if not quite forgotten, unawaited. A simple, repeated buzz would have told us what was happening but long-journey psychology knew that a cognitive response was not enough. Klaxon blasts, on the other hand, rip straight into the limbic system, by-passing thought and reflection for a fear-triggered raw reaction. In nanoseconds everything you need to deal with the emergency is up and running at optimal capacity. Eyes darting, adrenalin pumping, brain figuring at break-neck speed, the human animal is ready for anything that presents itself.

Hard to believe that that jarring acoustic hammering had not punched holes through the hull or jellied the higher life forms within; would not even be heard by whatever mutant pilot fish lived in our shadow. When it stopped, the silence of infinite, eternal space slumped back over us, like the onward rush of an avalanche momentarily halted in its tracks. But between the noise and its absence we were already on top of the problem. Like two blows from a sledge hammer on a half-filled drum, the fore and aft thrusters fired for three seconds, shifting us quickly out of danger. On the screen the crossing tracks which had set off the alarm no longer touched. Inter III would continue on its course and we would continue on ours.

It was a poignant moment, and not just because this was an artefact from Earth. We knew we were near; we could see it, and expected to see more of its twenty thousand bits of orbiting hardware. But all, except Inter III, were unmanned. Which added a special poignancy to that moment - we were just fifteen kilometres from other people, frozen corpses though they were.

When it happened they knew then there would be no going back. They would have seen it - a bird's eye view - and in the space of a week or so watched the clouds block out everything they could name, as though drawing a screen across scenes too horrible to witness. Against that same screen the prayers and entreaties of billions had smashed unheard by the so-called giver of life on the other side. It was from his heavenly domain that the end had come. They would have scanned the dark brown cover for a window, a fleeting glimpse of white or blue or green, a familiar contour, but scanned in vain. No signals would have come either, a sign that they still existed for someone. Their own signals went unanswered. Did they kill themselves? Drug themselves silly? Wait heroically till life leached slowly out of them? Perhaps they had left a log - the first pages in a firm hand, matter-of-factly chronicling their plight, then the beginnings of incoherence and a progressively illegible script as cold and $CO_2$ overcame them. Clear stuff or gibberish, no one will read it. Long before their technology - our technology - returns, they, their words and their craft will have burnt to a cinder in the fires of re-entry. Perhaps they already have.

\*

Everyone fell very quiet in the couple of hours after our near fatal rendezvous, more aware than ever that we were it. There was still no sense of movement, but now with Earth visibly growing in our port the sense of distances being covered rather than time endured returned, something we had last experienced almost nine months before as we pulled away from Mars.

Indifference - to us. That was the message we all felt Earth conveyed as we took it in turns to gaze upon its radiant, startling freshness. It was as though we had caught it in the moment of its becoming, seeing it rather than recognizing it, unmediated by memory or expectation. There it was, sedately spinning against the black ocean of space, a cosmic gifted child, idiot savant even, innocently oblivious to the exception - the life-sustaining, life-regenerating, sun-mastering, dazzling exception - it represented. It alone, of all those other diligently whirling concretions of rubble or gas - Mercury, Venus, Mars, Jupiter, Saturn, Uranus, Neptune, Pluto, and the two thousand seven hundred and eighty then known exo-planets - was a working bio-physical system, a home made for life by life itself.

*Life from space - that's what we represent*, said my mind, still then in cocky human mode. Panspermia, Arrhenius had called it in 1908, inspiring Hoyle later the same century, and a pioneering TV series called Quatermass, which I had read about but never seen. It was a neat idea, especially the Mars version, though proof was hard to come by:

Big impactor hits Mars three or four billions years ago;

Big impactor blasts off bits of life-containing Mars rock;

Life-containing Mars rock journeys through space;
Life-containing Mars rock bangs into Earth;
Extremophile bacteria like what they see;
Life starts.

Was this what Arrhenius' grandson had detected in the banded iron formations on bleak Akilia island, the oldest rocks in the world, just before the third millennium? Life which had begun just after, or perhaps even survived, the Late Heavy Bombardment, when giant meteorites rained down on Earth with an intensity never to be repeated? Was there a connection between that and us - we as a re-run of that first injection of life from a far planet, four billion years later? Or were those puzzling grains of carbonaceous matter, locked in their mineral matrix like an heirloom forgotten in its strong-box, the relics of a biota which we - what eventually became *we* - had wiped out and supplanted?

Whatever, Mars-born or not, three or four billions years later it had ended, again. At least our kind of life had ended. But our kind of life was irrelevant to Earth. If our readings were correct, the right kind had already emerged; maybe not the intelligent stuff, but the stuff which mattered, the Gaia-stuff, the stuff you could hardly see or not at all, the million-to-a-cubic-centimetre stuff, like the microscopic life-forms in our tonne of Earth soil we had brought back with us and which in the first days of Settlement had allowed us to kick-start life in a man-made biosphere, our tiny living pimple on the face of a dead planet.

Lovelock and Margulis had said it would survive. How else but by biotic activity could we explain that puzzling coexistence of methane and oxygen in the same atmosphere? The one cannot exist with the other, unless it's being continually replaced, and vice versa. And how else explain the paucity of carbon dioxide? The heavy slice of oxygen? Carbon dioxide will not go away, or oxygen exist, unless something is controlling the process. And the only thing that can do that is Earth's alone - life.

That great ripe ovum might or might not admit our speeding gamete, but if our ring at the door was ignored, only we were the losers, not Earth. Life would continue for another half billion years, with or without us, as it had done for the previous four, before finally relinquishing its hold as the dying Sun flared out to engulf the inner planets, Mercury, Venus, Earth…Mars.

\*

We could see the Moon as well. The Moon! So stately, so self-assured…and so distant from Earth, as though gravity had nothing to do with it and it was there because it wanted to be there, a free companion rather than a captive rock, a discerning visitor from elsewhere, and not, as we well knew, a receding fragment of Earth itself. A Moon-less Earth! At least we were not coming back to that. The first poem grandmother taught me came to mind. (Was that the start of my obsession with this Moon which didn't need a name?)

*Chuang qian ming yue guang*
*Yi shi di shang shuang*

*Ju tou wang ming yue*
*Di tou si gu xiang*

New myths would be born; beneath its gaze the same eternal sentiments would be exchanged and, on some still night another Li Bai, far from his loved ones, would look up from his lonely bed to the moon-frosted landscape beyond the window and think of home.

\*

Peaceful scene! It was not always so. After months on board with no horizon, not even the featureless, rubble-strewn nearness of a Mars one to take you beyond yourself, beyond the next bulkhead, beyond that knuckle-cracking, tunelessly humming, endlessly nail-biting, snuffling, nose-picking other - *Can you stop doing that! What?* - the membrane of civilization would sometimes rupture. It never seemed to get any thicker, any more resistant to the monstrous forms clawing at its nether side, and all too often breaking through.

They had realized that, at last; the light had finally penetrated the leather lantern. It took thousands of years before they accepted what they had already known for at least two hundred years: that the barbarism of the past was an ineradicable part of the present, because the human brain was the human brain and the dark parts of it would never go away. It could be controlled, but not by peace-keeping forces, embargoes, bombing campaigns and international tribunals, always a massacre too late. It was a huge leap for them to take, and a brave one (the conspiracy theorists had had a field day); and tragic that they could not have seen how well it would have worked on a larger scale than the few pilot applications allowed. It had worked in the Settlement to solve our relatively minor outbursts; and it had worked in our own eleven-man pressure cooker.

The breakthrough had come in 2115 with Das and Ondobo's work in neurogenetic pharmacology. With them, paradise-engineering entered the mainstream. It was they who re-encephalised the emotions, gave them an address in the brain. It was they who had finally pinned down which alleles of which genes regulated which post-synaptic cellular processes and the feel-good, do-good, be-good cascades they unleashed; they who had identified which substances would activate the right neurotransmitters to trigger the right sub-receptors to open the sluice gates. Their blue-print for life-improving, life-enriching new states of thought and emotion opened up breathtaking new perspectives for enhancing our humanity. No more mindless *turn on - tune in - drop out* dependence. A loving world no longer seemed the obscene dream the banalization of evil had made it. From empty piety, loving thy neighbour had become, would soon have become, a biological reality, as Pearce had said it would a hundred and fifteen years earlier in his then little known paper.

The vile, unspeakable nastiness - individual or collective - of sick, cruel emperors, of dictators, of Mengeles, Pol Pots, Simbas, Police Batallions, Intera Hamwe, Klansmen, the Wonderlanders, Kill-Gen, of knee-cappers, racists, torturers, executioners, rapists, ethnic cleansers, Geneticos, Enraptors, Dawn-5, the 27-27, of the Heavenly Twins, was on its way out. The better angels were coming. The post-human world was just around the corner. Frightening? Yes, but what a challenge!

*

God knows what a visitor would have thought of us as he floated through the connection tunnel, had we had one. We were still humans, still *homo sapiens*, despite our Martian background. A one-on-one comparison between a Settler and someone who had always lived in Earth gravity would have revealed no obvious anomalies. But look at eleven Settlers and eleven non-Settlers and differences began to emerge. I mentioned before the longer legs, the bigger chests, the taller stature generally. We weren't stick insects; we walked on two legs and gestured with our hands, but there was a spring in our movements, as though our contact with the ground, while essential to our ability to walk and run and sit just like any other human, was not so determining. We couldn't fly; we weren't birds either, but lighter gravity gave us an airiness, a lightness, a sense of autonomy which I realized I had lost forever that very first day when, crawling over the sill of the open hatch into the shallow surf, I felt two invisible clones of myself pressing down on my back.

But after almost nine months of zero G, our virtual visitor would have had to be blind not to see what a strange crew we had become. Our longish legs had turned spindly as hydrostatic pressures ceased to operate and fluids shifted upwards; our faces were correspondingly puffy above bulging neck veins, and our chests more voluminous than ever as lungs and heart, unmoored by weightlessness, floated freely in a relaxed rib cage. Kidneys, liver, spleen, stomach and intestines, similarly liberated, added an ungainly bulge to our bellies while vertically we were taller, another five centimetres at least, our spines released from gravity's vice.

And those were just the visible changes. Internally we had lost bone calcium; our plasma and electrolyte levels had gone down, and our muscles had atrophied, even changed their nature as fibres within them, essential in gravity, found themselves with nothing to do. *All reversible effects*, we had been told before we left. But while we thought little of it in the initial stages of our trip, at that stage in the journey, just a few days out from Earth, the possibility that physically we might not be able to cope started to…weigh on us.

There would be no welcoming ground crew or state-of-the-art medical attention; we did not even know whether the programme was going to land us where we had planned. Or if it did, that some band of crazed survivors would not take one look at us as we stumbled, pale and gangly, into the blinding light of that big sun and hack us to pieces before we could slam the hatch shut again. It sounds daft now, I know, but in space the mind itself is unleashed, just like the body.

\*

Injection minus 2 - just forty-eight hours to go before we took the plunge. We had been in Earth orbit for several days. Below us, before us, as far as the eye could see, stretched the whirling white and blue envelope of Gaia, Lovelock's "dappled sapphire". We watched a small meteor confidently streaking towards it and kidded ourselves we heard its muttered expletive as the invisible, resistant air bounced it off its tracks. I thought of that first bee again, banging into the dome. In two days we would thrust our way through that deceptively pregnable barrier and just a few minutes later, but a world away from where we had come from, float down on our triple parachutes to either the end or the beginning of our journey.

Even Xing was aware of the moment. The stupor from which he had intermittently emerged at longer and longer intervals over the last few weeks, seemed suddenly to evaporate. It was as though he had tapped into that pulsing source of life, felt some aura which even as we orbited was enclosing us in its net. It was easier to see things on the monitors but he insisted that we get him to the port and let him experience the sight directly. He would get down alive, just; we felt sure about that then, but afterwards? We had no illusions. But in that moment, he was no different from us all. We were the last recipients of that blind stare which, just over two hundred years ago, had humbled the first men on the moon and all who later experienced it at second hand.

Like the imprint of an invisible fingertip testing for dust, we saw the shadow of the sun-eclipsing moon moving across the globe. We saw *"how swift, how secretly, the shadow of the night comes on"*, the unforgiving onslaught of the terminator, routing the day from pole to pole. We saw, in greens and blues, reds and yellows, of unearthly intensity, the polar aurora shimmering and feinting, flapping and fluttering, to a magnetic rhythm only they could hear. And on the dark side of the earth, we watched fields of cloud a thousand-kilometres long glowing momentarily as exploding blooms of lightning flowered within them. At sunrise, heralded by a stab of brilliant blue, like a sword slicing into the Earth, we saw the same clouds transformed into a rippling expanse of molten copper, and not just once a day but every ninety minutes, and never tired of looking. But of the glowing lights of cities and highways, there was no sign; no electronic fingers reached up to welcome us home; no wakes criss-crossed the oceans; no sunlight glinted off a fuselage.

\*

As we orbited in those few days before landing, it was like seeing someone you knew, recognizing them straightaway but knowing that something - but what? - had changed. Ah ha! You've lost the moustache! Your hair, it's shorter! New eyeglasses? The Americas were still there, the two trapeze artists, someone had once called them, ready to fly off in opposite directions but for that life-saving grip on Central America. Yet something was not quite right. There was a roundness, an exaggerated incurving, to that south-eastern seaboard of North America which was not there before. Not that we had ever seen it, but we knew the maps. The Florida panhandle had gone, and much which lay to the west of it was now sea. The Appalachians seemed nearer the coast than before, but it was not they which had moved And the bar of the trapeze itself seemed pitted, eaten into, almost, but not quite, fractured.

Eurasia was still there, and Africa and the Indian sub-continent and Australia, but all disconcertingly different. For a start, there seemed to be more sea. It had always been there, the ocean around us, the Pacific, the Atlantic, the Indian Ocean, the three ragged petals of that gigantic bloom curving up from the Southern Ocean. "Earth" was a misnomer for a planet seventy percent water, but later even more so. We could see what once had been a long, leaf-shaped island ninety kilometres off the coast of China, now shrivelled to a mountain chain peeking above the waves. On the mainland, Tai Shan, the holy mountain, still soared, but above an island. South-East Asia was unrecognizable.

Small islands dotted the seas of Europe's north-western seaboard; Scandinavia was almost an island. Tentacles of blue, some sinuous, some broad and stubby, were feeling their way inland on the northern shores of an expanded Mediterranean whose African shore had receded south, further from Europe. The sub-continent was thinner and sharper; its north-eastern coast longer by several hundred kilometres where Bangladesh had once been. Africa had lost its substantial profile; dented and breached, it looked deflated, like a punctured balloon.

But it was not just the shapes which had changed. High in the northern latitudes, Greenland, once Earth's biggest island, had lost its perpetual whiteness; its ice-cap, already terminally eroding, had finally gone and where once there was one large island, there were now three, and innumerable smaller ones. We could see ground and vast patches of light green. Further to the south-east, Nunavut was free of snow and ice, and just as green. I remember checking the date - this was Earth-calendar April, the beginning of the thaw, but there was nothing to thaw. On another pass we saw Siberia, its western expanse a vast sheet of water, and its four mighty rivers, still flowing northwards, but into a liquid sea. The frozen Arctic was no more. A handful of raggedly-shaped ice islands tens of kilometres long were drifting in a slow, anti-clockwise gyre into the Greenland Sea and thence south past Iceland to the Atlantic. There, earlier remnants - we counted eleven of what, if we could see them so clearly, must have been the biggest of them - were slowly shrinking to extinction in the warm seas of post-impact Earth.

And at the other end of the world a ragged patchwork of white, black and green, split into two unequal areas by a massive mountain chain, had replaced the frozen monotony of Antarctica, a sight not seen (had anyone been there to see it), for fifteen million years. A huge lake glinted dully in the sun, the mysterious Lake Vostok perhaps, whose discovery beneath three kilometres of ice had so excited late $20^{th}$ century scientists, keen to see in its cold-loving bacteria a slender ray of hope for life on Mars. From one of the small land masses in the west of the continent, smoke was drifting westward. For a moment our hearts quickened - *There are still people down there*! - before we realized that no camp fire, not even a blazing forest, could produce a plume of those dimensions. We followed the trail back to its thinnest point and saw the volcano. In the sea, plankton blooms hundreds of kilometres long, drifted milky green against the darker water around them. At least one life form had survived. If there was one, there had to be more.

And what changes! We knew then that Earth was not the Earth we had read about. For the first time on our journey, the possibility that the vital parameters might have shifted nagged at our minds. Thirty-five degrees, even forty was one thing, but what about the air? We knew there was still oxygen, and still quite a lot, but the range was critical If oxygen fell below 15% we could make no fire; if it rose above 25%, one lightning strike, one red hot dollop of magma from a restive volcano, and we would be burned alive, however much greenery there was. Maybe it would be more insidious. There would still be life-sustaining oxygen, but less than before, making any effort at sea-level as tiring as working five thousand metres above it.

Death by disease was more likely. Even on still peopled Earth, the rising temperatures had pushed dengue fever and malaria into once cool highlands and safe temperate climates. People in Europe slept under mosquito nets. But it was the numbers which were important. One epidemic of just twenty victims, or just the females wiped out, or the males, and that was it - our two-seconds worth would be over, and no one would come afterwards to know. It would be as though we had never been.

*

A new restlessness had taken over. We were almost there. But first, there was cleaning time, a mundane house-keeping exercise to make those long hours pass more quickly. Nothing was supposed to be left undisposed of, but the path of least resistance (human propensity for) meant that more often than not the detritus of bodily processes - stray hairs, eyelashes, boogers, toenails, crusty prills of earwax, the sloughed off soles of feet not needed for walking - never made it to the waste sacks. Over nine months a single human nose yields enough dry snot to fill a cup, an ear enough wax for a sandwich. *(So gross!* the children would exclaim in joyful horror, on the enth retelling of this much requested detail.) For a few hours the tiring drone of the vacuum cleaner could be heard all over the ship, sucking out the forgotten fruits of endless boredom from wherever they had got to. Gravity would soon return. I wanted it to be an experience we would all remember, unsullied by the pitter-patter of desiccated pickings falling from the filters and wherever the air currents had pushed them.

We cut our hair short, shaved our beards off and, for the last time, marvelled at the gobs of water, jelly-like but quite unsticky, clinging to our skin as we gave ourselves a final rub-down. Soft fur had grown over my butt, as it had on many of the others' unused rear ends, and knees, and even backs, a harmless but mirth-inducing sprouting which quickly disappeared after a few days in gravity.

*Pity none grew on your head*, said Szeto, running her hand affectionately over my hairless scalp.

The hab had never been so uncluttered. That humble task had been important - a ritual cleaning, like our home-cleaning that now marks the end of the Arctic night; it showed the past was over; the future was waiting for us, just a few hours ahead.

A dull clunk and we knew that the heat shield had deployed. Instructions glowed on the screen. Crew took their positions, belted up, apprehensive at this sudden change of cadence. Time-scales shifted brutally from months to minutes; distance took on meaning again. Hearts beat faster. There was a flutter of nervous banter; lights dimmed; and then a long silence, perhaps only five or ten minutes but it seemed longer. Then a surge as the boosters fired, briefly, followed by the slightest of tremblings and a bright glow on the monitors. The trembling got worse. I was reminded of ice-boarding over a badly maintained freeze-path - an image no sooner in my mind than gone again as the buffeting intensified. The screen went blank; we seemed to be plummeting out of control but all the readings said otherwise. My knuckles were white. I slackened my grip but tightened it again as the shuddering increased. We sliced down through the thickening layers of atmosphere. Enveloped in an impenetrable cocoon of ionizing gas, we had entered the dead zone, where no signals could get in and none out. But we knew we were alone; we knew there was no ground crew anxiously waiting for that first burst of static, no circling choppers readying for splashdown. Seconds stretched into minutes and then the screen began to clear. For the first time in nine months I could hear noise, external noise. Weight, thicker and denser than anything I had experienced before, oozed oil-thick back into my body. I lifted my left arm; instead of staying where I stopped, it flopped back to the support, a limb of lead. A small nut which had escaped the vacuum's reach, clanged down onto the deck, momentarily startling me. Then the outside roar dried up, like someone slowly turning off a shower. I was aware of the tops of my thighs pressing against the straps. We were plunging, straight down. There was a moment of panic, a jerky turning of heads as frightened crew searched for a reassuring glance. Arms, still unused to their new weight, reached out to touch a neighbour.

*Wait for it, wait for it, wait for it*, I heard myself intoning.

Then...*Whump*! The chutes opened, invisible above us, and it was over! Slowly, as if cushioned in a giant's palm, we sank Earthwards. No one spoke.

In minutes we would step out onto the planet.

# The New Beginning

It was early in the morning we heard it - a distant, slashing sound from somewhere to the back of us. Slash - silence - slash - slash…slash - silence - slash; each time over a hundred cuts - that's what they sounded like - within a fifteen-minute period. All of us had rushed outside, aware that this was not one of the normal noises of our new environment. Rain pattering off leaves was a new noise, wind combing itself through the grasses was a new noise, the muffled crash of waves on the rocky beach was a new noise, but after a few days we felt we had known them forever.

But that noise was different and sent all of us tumbling out of sleep into the clearing, necks strained this way and that trying to get a bearing. Zhudi jabbed east-south-east, pointing past the hillock where, cursing their new weight, we had lugged the still unassembled struts and blades of a generator. In the terra incognita beyond, a dense sapling wood swayed in the morning breeze. The noise was either in there or further away. It was its intensity which disturbed us.

Five of us went to investigate. We carried sticks and one flare. This was something new for all of us. At the Settlement we had known what to expect, but here was different - the unknown was everywhere. Even walking was different, feeling the wind rumpling your hair, moulding the clothes to your body, evaporating your sweat. Living in that thick, swirling air was like living in an incredibly clear liquid. We slurped it down greedily, for the first time in our lives free of cylinders, scrubbers, pressure suits, time limits and the ever-present threat of suffocation. But what of new threats?

As we moved forward I was conscious that we were leaving half the group behind - our first separation in nine months. We waved from the top of the first rise and then they disappeared from sight as we went over the crest and started picking our way down through the saplings. We stopped from time to time to listen again. Nothing. After half an hour we felt we had gone far enough. It seemed unlikely that the noise had come from so far away. Yet we had seen nothing en route.

Then I heard something I shall never forget, like nothing I had ever heard before, a low throbbing tone, as though from some primitive wind instrument, but within it, woven through it, of it but separate, two (or was it three?) shining rods of sound of an intensity and timbre which, I thought, could only be electronic in origin. We listened entranced and not a little frightened, crouched down like cavemen, sticks swung back ready to strike, hearts thumping. We waited, silently. The sound continued for a few minutes then cut, as though a switch had been thrown, and all we could hear was the rustle of the leaves in the trees and the crackle of dry stalks at our feet.

Slowly we got up and started moving forward again. In front of us the saplings gave way to a thick patch of bushes covering a gentle rise. The sound came again, from somewhere off to our left. Gomez and myself got down on all fours and started crawling, head-down, into the bushes, trying hard not to disturb the low canopy. It was hot work After five minutes we were both covered in sweat and bleeding from innumerable small scratches. As we came up to the top, the bushes started to thin. We looked at each other.

*Go!* said Gomez.

I straightened up, raising my head slowly above the ground cover, aware that the sun was right in my eyes and that I was breaking every rule in the book. Before us lay a lake, glittering in the early morning sun. Close in to the bank were clumps of rushes and little grass-tuffeted islands no more than a metre across. But it was what we could see further out which held us transfixed. Two rounded shapes were moving slowly over the surface. I ducked down and gestured to Gomez to move round to our left, nearer the end of the lake where I could see a big rock. That way we would have the sun at a better angle, and more cover.

The going was much easier and within minutes we had reached our target. And there, from the shelter of that moss-covered boulder, we saw what it was and knew what the slashing noise had been. Heads cradled between their hands, their faces almost in the water, in a gesture reminiscent of my maternal ancestors at prayer, two figures drifted across the lake on a flimsy raft of cut branches. I could see no lines, or baskets with fish in them, no pile of bait, no tethered bird waiting to plunge. They were not fishing. They seemed to be scrutinising the depths, methodically criss-crossing the three hundred or so metres from bank to bank as though searching for something lost. We watched, yes, in awe; heard the man speak to the other shape; heard her reply, higher pitched but no less abrupt, and saw them pitch down and peer into the dim waters again, heads together, hands clamped against their faces.

*

We hadn't expected company. There were not supposed to be any human survivors, anywhere. How could there be? Yet life, the non-human kind, impermanent but tenacious, would survive, had survived, we knew that. It has already survived at least thirty such impacts since it first appeared over four billion years ago. It was all around us - seeds, propagules, microbes, fungi, algae, bacteria, perhaps even beetles, small rodents…Over thirty-five years enough had survived to re-prime the faltering machine before it had stopped entirely. Except it wasn't a machine, nothing as simplistic as that.

The geneticists had learnt that lesson early on. You could develop plants to resist the cell-smashing cold of Mars, the relentless radiation, the bone-dry conditions, the feeble pressure, but one plant, even a whole field of them, even a whole hemisphere, could not make a planet live. Not without that special coupling which only a critical mass of life could set in place.

A viable temperature, viable salinity, a breathable atmosphere - all were artefacts of a bizarre evolutionary partnership between the rocks and seas of Earth and a thin patina of life forms, one billionth its mass. What breathes in the $CO_2$ breath of the worlds' volcanoes and keeps us from death by heat and suffocation? Life. What keeps the relentless inflow of salt to the seas from turning them toxic? Again, Life! And not even a visible part of it: the site of $CO_2$'s removal is a cell membrane less than a tenth of a micron thin. From that microcosmic activity a macrocosm is born - the living Earth, the geo-biological miracle which is Gaia. No other planet has oxygen, and chemistry alone could not maintain it.

S*mell the air, that'll tell you if life exists on Mars,* Lovelock had told Nasa over two centuries ago.

\*

We headed back, crawling at first, but once over the brow of the hill, running upright through the bushes oblivious to the thorns snagging our clothes and the boulders cracking our shins and knees.

*People,* we gasped, *people on a lake.*

*How many? Friendly? Did they see you? Did you speak to them? What did they look like? Doing what? Was that the noise?*

We were - "prejudiced" would be too strong a word - wary, was perhaps a better description of our attitude to our fellow humans, none of whom we had had any experience of, though we knew plenty about their world and how different it had been from ours.

*What do we do? They'll find us if we don't find them.*

Somehow, having seen them, that didn't seem a big risk to me, or even a risk at all. They certainly hadn't seen us but I wondered then, if they had, what difference it would have made. What they were doing seemed to engage their entire attention. There was an obsessiveness in their actions which excluded the immediate environment, as though nothing unrelated to their strange ritual could impinge on them. Hadn't they heard us land? Seen us dropping through the sky? Spied us stumbling and falling up the beach from the shallow surf where our hab had come down? Or covertly watched us a day later as, still labouring under our tripled weight, we engaged in our own ritual, the burial of Xing?

*I don't think so. Let them know we are here, and then leave them,* I said.

*Don't all go at once. Gomez and I will go back first, and then we can all meet them.*

Even then I was pretty sure they were no more than two.

We walked back up the hill, not bothering to hide, and when we came to the top and looked down once more on the lake, stood there, arms raised, hands wide open, waiting to be seen.

They spotted us. I saw the man's head turn our way and then back to the woman. She looked up. Even at that distance I thought I could detect a movement of fear.

Both arms still in the air, unthreateningly, smiling, we stumbled down through the bushes to the lakeside. First contact! Scenes from long unseen pre-mill movies flashed briefly through my head.

*We come in peace for all mankind.*

The extra-terrestrials - that was us, but we were no aliens.

The raft had drifted into the shallows. The man's feet were in the water and he was straightening up, slowly, a little stiffly, as he waded towards the bank. He gazed at us for a few seconds before his arm went up. He did not appear to be frightened. He turned and waded back into the water, grabbing hold of the woman's sleeve to bring the raft right into the shore. We drew closer.

*Hello!* I called.

I'd thought of *Greetings* but it seemed too grand, too pompous, even if they didn't understand a word I was saying. It might have been a momentous moment for us but the man seemed almost indifferent to our presence, unlike the woman. With her left hand she was holding up her long skirt, still dripping wet round the hem, and with her right discreetly pulling on the man's arm. I noticed she had a slight limp. She was nervous, ready to run.

What language did these people speak? How could we communicate? They both had high cheekbones. Their hair was gray - they were elderly - but as I studied their faces, I couldn't imagine it having been any other colour than black, for their eyes were almond-shaped and their complexion distinctly Asian. An image of my own grandmother flitted across my mind.

*Nin hao,* I said, not really expecting a burst of Chinese, but it seemed more appropriate.

*Atilitak,* replied the man. That's what it sounded like.

*Atilitak*, repeated the woman, whose grip on his arm had tightened.

The man was looking at us, uncurious, as though waiting for us to dismiss him. I pointed at Gomez and myself and then, raising eight fingers, back to the hill. Then I pointed up to the sky and back down to the ground. They looked at each other, quietly exchanged some words, and then back to us. Gomez made eating movements with his hand. Again an exchange. The man pointed towards the far end of the lake.

*Kaklatatuk!*

I nodded. He didn't smile but spoke to the woman who seemed to relax a little at his words. A brief gesture - he was going to show us his home.

\*

As we walked behind them, I noticed that both carried a small object at their waist, which they kept touching, as though checking it was still there. Little dried pods hung loosely from what looked like the skull of a small bird. A tightly plaited hank of dried grass bound round with some threads served as the body of the structure. From its lower end small pieces of bark swung on a loop of dried sinew between thin slivers of bone or horn. The whole thing was about six centimetres long.

We had been gone at least an hour.

The lake couple, as we came to call them, strode on at a steady pace. They were both light and wiry and must have been aware of the efforts Gomez and myself were making to keep up, gasping behind them under the leaden pall of our new weight. But only once did they look round to see if we were still there, as if not looking might make us go away as quickly as we had appeared.

We had turned away from the lake and into a narrow gully. Overhead the blue sky, that same blue sky which had beckoned us on across those dismal distances, showed patchily through a mesh of criss-crossing branches and overhanging grasses. And then we emerged into a small clearing, eyes crinkling against the strong sunlight. In the rock face off to our left was an opening. Before it, between two poles, a dozen or so small, shrivelled carcasses dangled from a line in the warm air. Some tubers lay scattered on the ground. On a nearby rock, neatly sliced disks of the same plant had been spread out to dry. Black pincers littered the ground.

*Masatakuk!* The man had unhooked two of the carcasses and, one lying in each palm, was approaching us. The woman had disappeared.

*Thank you! Thank you!* I said, smiling and nodding as I stepped forward to receive his gift. Gomez followed. We looked at each other.

*Meat.*

He read my thoughts as easily as I read his.

*Eat*, I said, remembering that even for my distant Muslim ancestors, the Book allowed you to eat taboo food if the constraints were right. We weren't believers but we knew that our Singerite upbringing, which on our meat-free former home had put no temptations (that strip of biltong apart) in our way, was going to be tested to the limit on our new one. We were not starving and not being threatened with death if we didn't eat the, whatever they were, some kind of rodent. Yet an almost inborn desire to meet the other half-way, not to be hostile or assertive, told us to get on with it.

I tore off a hind leg and nibbled on what I could find of a thigh. Gomez pinched the breast between finger and thumb, removing the thin layer of flesh above the shattered rib cage. We stood there, religiously chewing the smoky meat, and growingly aware that this was only the first course. The old man had gone over to the rock and scooped up a handful of the drying disks. Sliding them onto a large leaf plucked from a nearby tree, he was coming over again.

*Masatakuk!*

More smiles, more nods.

We ate on, the chewy rodent meat mixing with the powdery paste of the tubers which seemed to dry up all the saliva in your mouth. I was already on the last limb when the woman came back. To our relief we saw that she was bringing us some water. Leaves again, but this time big ones, furled into a cone to hold a good half litre of the stuff which I gulped down with the avidity of a stranded Settler gulping down the rescue crew's oxygen.

*Come back with us*, I signed, *we'll show you where we live.*

His hand came up, palm outward.

*No.*

I gestured towards the cave. The man put his palms together and brought them up to his cheek. I understood the message:

*Just for sleeping.*

He made no movement to show us what was inside.

*Is there anybody else around*? I signed.

He shook his head. The woman was busying herself with some branches on the other side of the clearing.

*Well, we're over there, whenever you want to visit,* I gestured again.

*We have tools,* I said, making digging motions in the earth. He pointed to a rusting machete propped against the rock.

I drew a lightning flash in the air and, twisting my face in mock pain, jerked my index finger back from an imaginary wire.

*Electricity as well, soon.*

A faint smile played across his lips, as though to say:

*I hear you and thank you for your concern, but we are not interested.*

*Pills?* Grimacing, I held my stomach, palmed a handful of imaginary capsules into my mouth, and mimed relief. He tapped the little bundle of bark and bones at his waist and shouted across to the woman. She straightened up and looking round to face us, made the same gesture.

The faint smile again; we were being dismissed. Time to go. At least there was no hostility.

Raising our hands in farewell, Gomez and I turned and re-entered the covered gully. I remember wondering if next time we came it would still be there. Or would I be like the poor fisherman in Tao Yuanming's tale grandmother used to tell me. Not a covered gully but a narrow fissure in the cliff face. He'd tied up his skiff and gone through…into a peach garden, a richly fertile valley of fruit trees and sparkling rills running between crop-filled fields. Everyone was happy, well-clothed, and in need of nothing. He stayed for a while, marvelling at this other life so close to his own bleak existence, and then gone back the way he'd come, to bring the others. But he never found the opening again. Strange reversal. We had everything but they seemed to want for nothing. What secret drove them to refuse what we had to offer?

We were almost through the gully when we heard the noise again. We stopped in our tracks. It was coming from behind us, the lake couple's camp. There were two sources this time, one much lower than the other, but again the same intertwined rods of crystalline sound above the low drones. It was difficult to walk quietly without snapping something under foot but slowly we tracked our way back till we were within a couple of metres of the clearing and still invisible from outside.

It was them. Face to face, noses almost touching, the lake couple were singing their music of another world. We stepped closer. Could they see us? We were already in the open but still they went on, their heads bobbing up and down in an insistent, relentless rhythm. They seemed in a trance, lifted out of their own existence to some elsewhere to which we had no access. We watched - five, ten, fifteen minutes - but there was no let-up and finally we left, unnoticed. Their singing followed us into the gully till, just before we emerged from the other end, it stopped. We walked back along the lake and up through the bushes again and down the other side to the others.

*

In the weeks that followed we all made the acquaintance of our elderly neighbours. Singly or in twos and threes (we felt all ten of us would be too much), we went back along the lake and into the gully - it was still there - and I think managed to convince them, especially the woman, that we were not going to disturb them or enter their lives and that this first visit was simply a courtesy call. Of course, it was more than that. We were intensely curious about them. How had they survived? Who were they? Our humanity apart, we had no common language or culture, but at least we seemed to share a sense of mutual respect. And if their hospitality seemed pre-programmed and lacking in warmth, little caring whether the object of its administration appreciated it or not, it was a lot better than outright rejection.

Then something happened which made me think that I had been wrong, and that their apparent indifference to us was just that - apparent - no more than a primitive force-field to keep them from dangers they might not be able to handle, just as some people use an endless stream of banter to stop you getting too close to their fragile core.

Ling had been out chopping wood, or rather chain-sawing wood to build more shelter. (What effort we had put into making that piece of equipment before we left!) By that time one of the generators was up and running and Earth's thick winds were keeping us supplied with a steady source of electricity. He had gone out with a fully-charged power-pack to cut down some of the older saplings over to our south. When he didn't come back by midday we started getting worried. The site was a mere ten minutes away and three of us were over there in no time. We saw what had happened immediately. He must have slipped, probably had his foot on a damp branch to support himself, and brought the saw down on his thigh. He had had the presence of mind to use his shirt as a bandage to staunch the copious bleeding but was very pale and near to passing out.

Quickly we got him back, aware that his wound was not a clean cut but a deep gouge. Flesh had been removed, making it very difficult to stitch the sides together. In the end we managed, though all of us then realised that this was the first time we had used our medical supplies and that if even small accidents were to occur with any frequency, the medical container would not last forever.

We ate supper as usual, Ling joining in the chat, though still very sore and weak. Next morning his temperature was 40 and climbing. By the end of the day he was intermittently delirious. By day three we knew what it was, and that it would get much worse. Neck spasms, jaw spasms, twitching face muscles - Ling had tetanus. By day five the spasms had spread to his back and chest. At times his whole body arched above the bed before collapsing back, totally exhausted. He was desperately scrabbling for breath and swallowing with difficulty. We debated whether to cut into his windpipe so he could breathe more easily (we were all aware that that wouldn't be his first time), but finally put it off, hoping that the drugs we were injecting into him would soon take over. We had had shots before we left but they were obviously no protection for that strain, or had lost their potency. But the penicillin and antitoxins didn't work either and the prospect of losing yet another of our band was too awful to contemplate.

Just like Thoreau's elder brother, I thought (there were passages of Life in the Woods I knew off by heart) - one day, the first of a new year as it happened, a young man with his life before him, sharpening his cutthroat on a strop, eleven days later dead from the insignificant cut on his finger he'd given himself in the process. That was over three hundred years ago but there we were, the citizens of the future, no better off.

*

The three of us looking after him all turned at the same time; we'd heard the swish of the door across the dry earth floor. The old man was standing there, a horn cup in his hands. Steam was rising from it and the hut was filled with an odour we had never smelt before, of roots and bark and dried pods and sap and flower heads, boiled to a dark brew. None of us sought to stop him. We knew our means had failed. The old man approached the bed, pulled a thick tube from his waist, a dried reed or stem, and sucking up a small amount of the liquid, gently dribbled it into Ling's mouth after holding it for a minute or two for the heat to go out of it. Ling gagged and then relaxed a little. Another spasm shook him, and then when it was over, another dribble of the infusion. After an hour he'd taken all of it.

Then, out of his bag, the old man took a thickly woven halter. He put it over his head and tugged it into place. On each shoulder there was a small wooden mask, one round-faced, one long-faced, but both with the same expression, at one and the same time solemn and mischievous, like someone trying to keep a straight face; on the chest a woven icon of some kind, a feminine form, but otherwise quite featureless, bar the eyes, which stared blankly ahead. Next, he put on a cap. Broad, boldly coloured stripes of orange and yellow and a dull green came down from the crown to join the intricately plaited band around his head. Then a dull, rattling sound. In front of his eyes, suspended from the headband, a face curtain of woven plaits strung with beads covered the top half of his face, revealing only his mouth and chin. He turned towards Ling again.

*Hotarie...Hotarie...Hotarie...*

Three times, then a pause...

*Hotarie...Hotarie...Hotarie...*

And all in a quietly pleading tone, as though asking someone behind a door if he was indeed there and if he was, to kindly unlock it and let him in. For a least a quarter of an hour the same word hypnotically repeated, then the tone changed, and the old man began to chant.

It was a low, rapidly-spoken chain of words, more conversation than mantra from its tone, rising and falling in a narrow range. Untouched at first, we slowly felt ourselves drawn in, unable to resist, like dropping off at table after a day's digging in the sun. We watched, amazed, its calming effect on Ling. The spasms were less frequent and less violent. He seemed to be breathing more easily and his forehead no longer burned so intensely. The one-sided talking went on and again I had that feeling that the old man was somewhere else.

*Take a rest,* I begged him, pulling back on his bony shoulder.

*You must be exhausted. Our friend is much better now.*

No response. The intense vocal effort did not seem to tire him, as though the voice came through him rather than from him.

Deep into the night he continued, not even sitting but half crouched, his knees slightly bent and his body leaning towards Ling.

When we awoke the next day, stiff and aching from the hard floor, the old man had gone and Ling was lying there, eyes wide open and flexing his wounded leg. No fever, no spasms, breathing normally and, he told us, *as hungry as hell.*

\*

After that there were no more facetious remarks about Adam and Eve II. That's what one of us had called them. Man had pushed his luck too far, went her scenario, and God had had enough, so down comes the impactor. And just to rub in the finality of it all, smirking from behind the clouds, God re-peoples his bruised and emptied Eden with this barren geriatric couple.

*And the first shall be the last! Ha! Ha! Ha!* he sniggers. *Enjoy!*

Claps of thunder more powerful than anything heard before shake the world to its solid iron core, the oceans disappear in a mighty puff of steam, and God heads off to another experiment.

We laughed at the time, irked (though we were slow to admit it) by our neighbours' indifference to who we were. But now the joke was on us. They had saved one of ours, reducing the probability, however fractionally, of our own extinction. And in the process ensured their own immortality. For they will live on. My children, our children, know every detail of that evening now. So will their children, and their children after them. There will be one day in the year when people remember that moment, celebrate what happened. We do already. That evening will be re-enacted, for thousands and thousands of years. Life-

Giving we call it. Little children will rush back early from school:

*Mama, Mama, I'm going to be Ling. I've got to twitch and look really ill. Qiang is going to be the Old Man. We have to make some syrup to dribble through the tube. I told him not to spit.*

There will be other parts as well - the Old Woman, and Gomez, and Han, and Zhudi, and poor old Xing and "The Settlers" (for those who can't remember lines) and lots of scenery to paint, lots of reddy brown for Mars, lots of green paper trees and grass for Earth. And a spaceship, all silvery and shiny, and "dappled sapphire" disks, about ten of them, in bigger and bigger sizes to show the Settlers getting nearer and nearer to Earth.

And perhaps more sombre moments as well, choirs gathered to sing to Mars, to the Settlers still there. Or already long disappeared.

*Shei zhidao?*

Who knows?

*

We learnt what was in the cave. The old woman had taken Zhudi in; she seemed at ease with her, though at that time signs were the only way they could communicate. Perhaps she reminded her of some long lost relative from the time before, a grand-daughter or a favourite niece.

Inside, the air caught at her throat. It was where they kept their fire, always alight, the smoke drifting up through a natural chimney in the rock to disperse unseen through numerous surface vents. The old woman had lit a bull-rush taper and swept it slowly across the inside walls. In its flickering light, a family of reindeer ambled across an ancient landscape; archers raised their bows to invisible targets; kneeling women gutted what must have been hares - you could see their big ears. Off to one side a masked shaman, his mouth only showing, girated and shook to the silent drumming of a line of dancing stick figures.

Pointing at the shaman, the old woman had taken Zhudi's hand, placed it on the small bundle at her waist and begun to intone an invocation, or so it seemed to Zhudi. The taper flared up and then spluttered out. Time disappeared, her surroundings disappeared and she and the shaman and the old woman were there together. She felt no fear. The air seemed crisper, colder. Half-heard sounds drifted through her mind - a distant trumpeting, a muffled shout. Beneath her feet the ground trembled, then stopped. Her mouth watered - a rich, savoury odour wafted past her nostrils. Close by there was a burst of high-pitched giggling, like children surprised; she could hear women talking softly, smell the pungent odour of half-cured skins. And then, suddenly, she felt very cold, colder than she had ever been before, buffeted by a wind with specks of ice in it which stung her face and made her throw her arms around herself and stamp her feet to keep warm. Out of the corner of her eye she saw the oily yellow flames of the taper the old woman was holding up to her. The shaman was still there, a small figure with his mask, just a drawing on a cave wall, back in his own time again with the reindeer and the hares and the archers.

Before they left the cave, the old woman gave her a little bundle of her own - bird skull, grass, bark, bone, sinew, thread. Outside in the warm sunlight once more, they had rubbed noses and patted the melting hail from each others' hair. And the old woman had laughed, knowing she was now safe from harm. (This from Zhudi - make of it what you will.)

\*

There were other contacts as well. The old man had come over one day, waited till a few of us had gathered round (by that time we had picked up a few words of his language; he himself was called Tubyaku) and then, reaching inside his clothing, had brought out a round black box.

*Kompas*, he announced. A familiar word.

He tapped the object with the long nail of his little finger. He set it down on the flat top of the boulder which marked the centre of the village, as we grandly called it, and lifted up the cover. Green letters I didn't immediately recognise spun back and forth on a black disk. It was indeed a compass. But we already knew what it showed. The day after we landed we had faced a problem. The antique ones we had brought with us (useless on Mars) had clearly shown the existence of a strong magnetic field. We had expected nothing else, except that the red-tipped needle, instead of pointing over the rocky outcrops to the beach, pointed in the opposite direction. We knew North was out there, over the sea. We'd seen the Plough. The pointers, Dubhe and Merak, still pointed at the Pole Star; there was no doubt on that score.

But we'd checked again, just to be sure, though we knew we couldn't be surer than that. A stick in the ground - mark the end of its shadow, wait ten minutes, mark the end of the shadow again, draw a line connecting the two marks and extend it past the second one. Left foot against the first mark, right foot against the end of the line - you're facing North. Simple textbook stuff. Yes, geographic North was still there, where we thought it was. But the poles had flipped - magnetic north had become magnetic south, or at least according to our compass. We had six; could they all be wrong? What could go wrong with a metal needle balanced on a pin? This was ancient Chinese technology - the ultimate in simplicity and reliability. But the doubt still lingered, till the day the old man came over.

*Severniyee*, he said flatly, almost apologetically, as though aware of the pointlessness of confirming a fact no one in their right mind would contest. Standing rigidly upright, right elbow tucked into stomach, right arm and index finger extended parallel to the ground, he pointed north towards the beach. Then he looked at the compass. On the arrowhead, the green C, the Russian S, for *Severniyee*, was pointing south. He looked back up to where he was pointing, down to the compass again and then at us, an expression of feigned puzzlement spreading over his face. He shrugged imperceptibly, bent slightly at the knees, and straightened up again, rapidly moving his lips left and right. A vague memory of a small figure with round hat and moustache rose from somewhere inside my mind and sank again. Unable to suppress a giggle (my first on Earth I remember thinking) I felt more relaxed than I had in a very long time.

Then he spun round and pointed in the opposite direction.

*Yozhnee!* He exclaimed, as though he had finally found what he had been looking for all his life.

*Yes, yes,* we all smiled back, infected by his clowning, and patting him affectionately on the back.

Y*ozhnee! South! Yozhnee!*

Mafala ran to her hut where our own compasses were kept and set one down next to Tubyaku's. We watched as the two needles quivered to stillness. All doubt was banished. *Zhinan ji.* Our compass, any compass, had become a south-pointer again. But this time it was for real, not just a matter of making one end of the needle more important than the other. *Nan.* South.

We already knew where we had landed - well within the Arctic Circle, almost right on longitude 116° East. To our north lay sea, the once frozen Arctic Ocean. To our south, frost-desert and tundra (what had once been frost-desert and tundra), endless mountain ranges, high, windswept grasslands, arid deserts, and then, thousands of kilometres from our primitive perch on this unfrozen new ocean, a softer landscape where a great civilization had once flourished - China. Down there lay, had lain, vast, teeming cities: Beijing, the northern capital...Nanjing, the southern capital... Guangzhou...and, where the sea started again, on the other side of Asia...Xiang Gang, the Fragrant Harbour, home of my great great grandfather. One day someone would make that trek, abseil down the line of longitude, down the side of the world to those distant names, following the south-pointing needle.

*

In the meantime coming to terms with our isolation, if isolation means anything when there is no-one left to be isolated from, is, I suppose, easier for us than any group of humans before. We had lived isolated - and under the threat of even greater isolation - all our lives. In the old mind-set it might look as though we had exchanged one periphery for another. Where we are now is on the very edge of the planet, about as far from the centre of things as you could have gone in the old world. On the fringes of a continent, barren tundra to the south, a frozen sea to the north; in winter, dark for twenty-four hours, in summer, cold, hostile to crops, this was the harsh homeland of a scattering of nomadic peoples, their cultures - Khatavam, Nganasan, Evenk, Dolgan Nyenets - almost as strange to us as a world from Borges. They lived on fish, seals, seabirds, whale, reindeer, berries, wild plants...and the organic pollutants and toxic metals of the industrial world, sifting down through the increasing haze onto the snow and ice and water of their once pristine landscapes.

But now it is different, or so we must suppose. We are the centre, by default. The ice has finally gone, the tundra has gone. To the north lies open sea, waiting to be crossed, to the south, a green wall.

*

And we are not as alone as we thought. Well, I only half go along with it, if that; my background is hard to overcome, but some of the others are more receptive - or should I say less ready to reject than they

141

would have been in the early days of our arrival. Most of them don't really *believe*, but it helps them to feel they belong, this grafting themselves onto the succulent, thick roots of others who had peopled this land for millennia.

We had no myths up there, none native-born at least. Some simple rites perhaps, were all we had, like corpse-wrapping, or even more mundane activities like digging a digester or pollinating a strip, which took on a symbolic meaning by reaffirming our shared identity. That, and some survival sagas every Settlement child knew by heart, a scattering of poems, the songs of Zenga Akitonde (which had enjoyed a brief cult following on Earth), our whirling cube dances, and a few polished chunks of olivine from the volcano lands. These were the meagre fruits of our almost two hundred years in that rubble-ringed oasis. Yet we treasured them and now even more that this is our contribution to the beginning of whatever is created here. (Well, perhaps not the cube dances, not in this gravity!)

But our neighbours' world has a texture and density we could never have imagined. Hotarie we knew about. Hotarie - the eight-legged reindeer stag, protector of man, and of our companion, Ling - we shall never forget. From Tubyaku and Neiming, we also learnt of the snow-white boy with the long nose and big eyes who could make himself invisible. And of the wolf-tailed boy, born to the childless woman. The shaman had told her to walk away from her tent and stand facing the moon. It was winter, the snow was thick on the ground. Hours went by, her legs were numb and her neck stiff with staring up at the endlessly pouring silver light. Then, almost fainting with cold, she saw the wolf in front of her. But it was walking away, tail high in the air. Its deep tracks were clearly visible in the snow - they came from between her legs and stretched back to the dark forest beyond the encampment.

There were even stranger beings, like Seimbytumu, who had no eyes but could see everything; Koubtumu who had no ears but who heard all there was to hear, and Nganabtumu, (the radio god Tubyaku called him) who had no mouth but told the shaman everything. When she was small my daughter was very frightened of them. She liked best the seven-tailed dog and the she-wolf with seven cubs. I have a charcoal drawing she did of them right here on the wood of my desk. My son preferred Mikulushka, the Iron Horse, with his thousand-strong army of stone men.

Barusi was even more frightening - a one-eyed, one-armed, one-legged zombie who was sometimes a helper and sometimes not, so you never knew where you were with him. But there were more trustworthy spirits as well, like the Frosty God and the Sun Mistress and the Water Mistress and the Tenth God. And they all had their helpers, the hornless reindeer, or the water-girl or the seven sun girls, whom they sometimes lent to you. Even the little creatures of the forest were not what they seemed; ermine, mice, stag beetles, all could be called on to get you out of a fix. At least they were still here, but the bears and the wolves and reindeer and dogs are gone for good, to us as familiar, yet as unknown, as dinosaurs to the people we have replaced.

The children loved to hear Tubyaku's hunting tales and what his dogs did, especially Noho, his favourite hunter, who had saved him from a bear, and how he'd met his pet reindeer years after a big storm had blown her shelter over and she'd run off into the forest. He was just about to pull the trigger when he heard a voice calling his name, not Tubyaku, but the name his mother called him when he was small, and then he realised who it was he had in his sights and lowered his gun.

From Neiming they learnt throat singing, the first human sound we had heard, and to throw their baby teeth into the fire. And from time to time Tubyaku would let them play with his drum and try on his headgear. The drum was made of reindeer hide, like the tents they used to live in, but there are no more skins, big ones at least. During one winter - now just one chilly unbroken night - he showed them how to make a miniature tent, using small patches of skin he'd saved from his rodents. Then they made their own. They were called *chum* and Tubyaku, remaining true to his promise, performed a tent-cleaning rite for them as soon as daylight returned.They thought it was just a game but then after two hours of chanting by Tubyaku and his total indifference to their tugs at his sleeve, they realised it wasn't a game for him. I told them later what had happened and what his life had been like before, but at that age they couldn't take it in.

He'd built a sled for them, which they could easily pull across the ground when they were small enough not to weigh much. I got some frost from the cold-room and told them how much faster it used to go on that, even if they were grown-ups and were carrying a big load. Our coming from Mars was difficult enough for them, without explaining about the impactor as well, and why there was no snow or ice any more.

\*

How did I feel about Tubyaku telling them of his hunting exploits, or his eating rodents for that matter? Would my children, our children start killing animals again? Strange, to me, to us, brought up in the Settlement, this coexistence of spirituality and killing. It was Tubyaku's profound respect for nature which had made communities like his - the Earth's indigenous peoples - the darlings of the industrialised world's environmentalists. Which did not stop the Greens from trying to deprive him and his people of meat, their only source of protein, by blocking their whale hunts and caribou shoots and seal cullings.

*Eat vegetables!,* they cried from their hi-tech inflatables, cosy in their synthetic weather-wear no plant could rival for warmth and durability. Yet they rejected the research into GM beans and corn which would have made it possible, and rescued millions of subsistence farmers from chronic poverty. Such crimes against humanity! Will the medieval re-emerge in our new world?

\*

We can't die out; a replacement rate is not good enough for us. We must grow. We will have to be very fertile to survive - at least five children per couple. It doesn't have to be that way; after all, we have what we need to control births, to cut out reproduction completely. In the Settlement we had zero growth; we had to have that, given our meagre resources. But here, our views have changed. It is no longer a question of let it happen or not. Here following the Dao may lead to a dead end. The tender indifference of the world is a challenge we cannot ignore if our being here is to mean anything. We lost Xing, we almost lost Ling. No, we are positively striving to make it happen.

Last month, within ten days of each other, our first grandchildren were born. My only son is the father of one, Gutierrez and Mafala's eldest son the father of another. Their companions are Inoue and Gomez's daughter and Kim and Szeto's, both seventeen. Our two daughters of Eve, we half-jokingly call them, the mothers of Humanity II. Forty-five thousand years from now (you see, sometimes I do believe it is going to happen), maybe sooner, a scientist will study the mitochondrial DNA of thousands of women from hundreds of millions more and group them into less than a dozen clusters. Isa and Jasmine will be the source of two of them, and their younger sisters and playmates of the rest.

One of the babies, my grandson, is Xing; for us, in memory of the eleventh member of our crew; for Tubyaku and Neiming, who see things differently, Xing himself.

*He has come back to you,* they told us.

The other baby, a girl, is Paktin, the *timbun* of their eldest daughter.

*We are happy now*, Neiming told me.

*Have more babies! We had four children - they are waiting for their timbun, and now I am too old.*

Thank God for Neiming - we had learnt the instructions off by heart, but she has the expertise; her hands had delivered tent-fulls of children. Her calming presence, and the tears of joy which rolled down her cheeks as she held little ones in her arms again, has made everything so much easier. Not so far into the future, if all goes well, we will be a community of great grandparents and great grandchildren.

*

So now, as my chronicle nears its end, eight years after I began it on those awful home-made sheets, there are twenty-nine of us: five Settlement couples, seventeen first generation Earth-born, and now two second generation.

No one has died since Xing left us. We buried him at the foot of a small slope facing north-north west across the sea to the distant hills of the island. He spent just eleven hours on Earth, propped up on a make-shift recliner we'd fashioned for him from chests and sacks of seed just a few metres from where he now lies. He knew he was going. He had told us what to do when he gave the signal, to make it easy for him. We took turns to sit with him as we unloaded what we needed for our first night. The hab had come down at a slight angle, one end resting on some rocks, but even without that awkward tilt, another night on board was something none of us would have considered. We had had enough.

Our first night on Earth was going to be spent in the open, free of protective walls and protective suits, voluptuously, and yet not a little masochistically, as we soon realised, experiencing the oppressive suck of its gravity. Just out of the hab, we had crawled, dizzy, nauseous and so very weak, through the low surf and collapsed face-down among the dried twigs and broken shells of the tide-line, arms and legs outstretched in an act at one and the same time of joyful possession and willing submission. We lay there, unmoving, as though charging our bodies with its force, surrendering ourselves to its overwhelming presence.

I watched a small shell move just a few inches from my head. Little claws scrabbled in the sand. I picked it up and instantly they snapped back inside. I put it down. Just an empty shell again, till once more it moved, and scuttled into a small rock pool. Life on Earth. I went back for Xing, still in the hab, and with great difficulty half carried, half dragged him out into the sunlight, into the glory of that first Siberian morning.

He died later that day as the irrecoverable colours of a magnificent sunset darkened into night. We left him there, settling down around him, as he had asked us to do, and buried him early on the second day.

*

That was one story we have told the children, as they will theirs. The story they told us was the answer to something which had mystified us from the very beginning - just how had Tubyaku and Neiming survived? We had all of us picked up a few words of their language as they had of ours but the mix was the poorest of poor pidgins and frustration rapidly set in when we tried to get onto anything not immediately identifiable in the surroundings or easily mimed. But the children had spent a lot of time with the old couple once we learnt that there was nothing to fear from them (and they learnt there was nothing to fear from us) and by the time they were four or five spoke as much Khatavam as English. They were our go-betweens. Yet it was not until they were just about in their teens, five or six years back, at the time when questions about identity and origin, about who they were in the wider scheme of things, started to surface in their newly self-conscious minds, that the bits and pieces of a story, as they thought it was, which they had been hearing over the years from Tubyaku and Neiming, began to coalesce, and the whole picture was finally spread before them.

*

We set off early one morning, around four, but the sky was as light as it had been when we had gone to sleep the evening before, the sun just about to climb again after its brief midnight dip below the horizon. Already the air was warming up, the humidity was tolerable and Tubyaku had assured us there would be plenty of water along the way.

There were seven of us - myself, my son Lijian then twelve, Mafala, her eleven year old daughter Isa, Szeto, Kim and Tubyaku himself. Leaving the village we made for the beach where, heavily barnacled, the hab still lay just as it had landed, one end up on the rocks, the other in the water. From its sloping underside a heavy curtain of dark green seaweed swung sluggishly to and fro in the low swell. We would follow the coast, literally at the sea's edge, round to our east and then cut across a hilly bit of country to the next bay and track round that.

Easier said than done - there were no roads, no paths, not even then. There was a river to cross as well and we spent a sweaty two hours building a small raft, just big enough for one. Tubyaku had told us to bring a length of our precious rope, the last of the synthetic coils we had not yet used and had kept for just such an eventuality. (The rest of the stuff we had brought from Mars was for lashing cabins together, keeping nets in rivers, pulling loads.) With a crude paddle, each of us dug our way across the sluggish current to the other side and then the others pulled the craft back with the rope for the next person. With two ropes it would have been quicker, one secured to the raft, and one stretched across the river to haul ourselves across on, but plenty of everything was something we didn't have, and wouldn't have, for a very long time to come. Now, of course, things are getting better. It was hard work but the excitement of what Tubyaku was going to reveal to us kept us going.

*

There was no communication with home; phones or radios were also not something we had, though we knew all about them and what was needed to make them. We knew what the future held, but that was all in the past. We had no infrastructure, technical, industrial, or commercial, and no human resources but our own. We did have three flares with us, so we could be located if anything went wrong, but once we had used them we couldn't replace them. Like our light-bulbs, our stock of them was already severely depleted. We did have Tubyaku, and I guess we had his invisible pals as well, but that was it.

We spent three nights in the open, sleeping with difficulty in the almost constant light, despite our tiredness. By eight on the fourth day we had almost reached the end of our trek.

No doubt was possible - it was man-made. Branching off a bend in the next river, a narrow waterless trench ran straight as an arrow for about three kilometres in a roughly southerly direction, stopping before what was obviously a continuation of itself, but one segmented every two hundred metres or so by a thick wall. From where we looked down on it, exhausted after our climb up the last hill, there was no mistaking the precision which had informed its construction. Even after so many years, the invading greenery could not camouflage the sharp angles of the concrete reinforcing which kept its vertical sides in place. But what Tubyaku was pointing at was not the trench itself but a distinct bulge in the vegetation just before the first wall, a sort of rounded spike which stuck up above it.

*Tembinaki!* We heard him say. *Still there*, as much to himself as to us. And then he began walking down the slope and we followed, the children in front with him, chattering away in Khatavam.

*Lodka!* He shouted over his shoulder as he reached level ground, *Lodka!* and started running towards the trench until thickening undergrowth slowed his pace and we caught up with him and our two. Through the trellis of branches we could see a matt black surface rising vertically from a narrow platform.

*We need to clear a way through*, my son told us, translating for Tubyaku, who was already untying the four machetes we had brought with us. It was not

151

difficult work - in ten minutes we had hacked an opening to the side of the trench and pulled aside enough of the natural cover to see what it was we had come to see.

*Lodka!* said Tubyaku, a trace of triumph in his voice.

He had jumped the metre and a bit from the edge of the trench to the flat top and was hammering the side with stock of his machete. We heard the dull sound of very thick metal reluctantly responding to his blows.

Tubyaku's *lodka* was the sail of a submarine, the rest of its hulking presence all but enveloped by the mud and vegetation and dead leaves which had accumulated around its massive hull over the past four decades. After an hour of slashing and hacking and pulling branch from branch we had cleared enough of the deck to find the hatch. The cover was open, prevented from sealing itself shut by a thickish branch which chance had blown across the metre-wide aperture when last it was used. We heaved it open, three of us straining against the weight which in its working days the hydraulics would have tipped open effortlessly. A metal ladder disappeared into the darkness beneath our feet. We had two crude flashlights - just a solar-charged battery with bulb and lense all held together in a bit of piping cannibalised from the hab - but they worked well. After a cursory sweep round the space where the ladder ended in a pool of murky water, we climbed down. Unhesitatingly, Tubyaku went forward, encouraging us on with his hand as though aware of our apprehension and anxious to put our minds at rest.

A burst of Khatavam from Tubyaku.

*They spent two years in here,* my son told us.

Tubyaku strode forward confidently, as though he knew the place with his eyes shut. Cable ducts and pipes ran along both sides of the narrow passageway, looping over what might have been doors or access panels, before finally disappearing into a bulkhead a few metres ahead of us. When we reached it and stepped over the raised rim of the oval aperture into the next compartment, Tubyaku had already gone into a small opening on our left and was beckoning us in. We found ourselves in a narrow storage area. A long line of shelves, the topmost well above head height, stretched for about 15 metres down one side, leaving us with just enough space to turn round.

*Borsch! Borsch! Borsch! Borsch!* Tubyaku announced with distaste, slapping with increasing violence the first four of the dozens of five-litre cans which still covered half the shelving.

*He hates the stuff,* Isa informed us.

I had guessed as much but was already thinking that a few cans of thick soup would be welcome booty to take back home and not just for the taste. (Too bad about the beef, I remember thinking. Not eating those chunks was not going to help any cattle - and anyway, there weren't any left) Dried vegetables apart, ready-to-eat food was a luxury we had not experienced since leaving the Settlement. There were a few rust spots but otherwise the containers seemed unbreached. (We were able to lug back a couple each without too much effort.)

We filed out of the soup store and followed Tubyaku down the length of the hull. Soon we were under the sail, in a wider, higher room lined with electronic panels. The bridge. Here the officers would have sat in their padded swivel chairs monitoring the instruments, checking the radar, adjusting the ballast to keep the craft steady as the detection array scrutinised the sea bed beneath them for mineral resources.

I checked the binnacle. North was South.

*I saw it change*, Tubyaku told Lijian. *Tell them*

*It took thirteen days. Just under fourteen degrees every day. Right after it happened.*

\*

And then the whole story came out. They had known it was going to happen, Even out there we had known it was going to happen. But between first detection and final impact fate had played a nasty trick on the world in the shape of an intense solar flare. And while not unexpected - they came in 11-year cycles and that was an eleventh year - was of an intensity and violence no one had foreseen. Overnight the global village collapsed; satellites went mute, television screens broke up, anti-missile defence systems went on malfunctioning, but differently, cell phones stopped working, power went off, radio waves no longer bounced back to Earth, the Mars-Earth link was broken, and Hubble V, which had been tracking Hofmeister and its baby since it first entered the solar system, stopped transmitting its coordinates.

Torino. By then every one knew the word, and the scale which went with it. Torino 0: events having no likely consequences; Torino 1: events meriting careful monitoring; Torino 2-4: events meriting concern; Torino 5-7: threatening events; Torino 8-10: certain collision.

Torino 8 had at least given hope to most parts of the world, already prepared for something bad by the transition from T7 to T8 as forecast after forecast confirmed the increasing danger. T8 was a collision capable of causing localised destruction only. That "only" was found so reassuring, but "only" was a small country wiped out, a megacity - Rio, Shanghai, Cairo - totally obliterated. It had happened before, in 1908. But there had been no city beneath the air blast, just reindeers, a river called Tunguska, and a great swathe of Siberian forest. With any luck it would be somewhere else, not their backyard.

But then came the upgrade to T9, and the threat of regional devastation, a continent-sized catastrophe. Even then hope remained - there were five continents, and one of them might be Antarctica, so the odds were still okay, and if it was Antarctica, never mind the accelerated rise in sea level which further melting of the ice would bring, or mile-high tsunamis sweeping north (the southern hemisphere would bear the brunt) and months of dark and cold; at least some of humanity would survive.

And Tubyaku and Neiming in all this? No magic had saved them, none of his helpers had pulled a fast one on the laws of physics (I was relieved to hear him say this - he didn't put it that way, of course); it was enough that this reindeer herdsman was also a shaman for a chain of perfectly explicable and untoward events to occur to bring him and his wife into the unassailable security of the lodka.

Many of its crew were locals, Khatavam or half-Khatavam and, russified or not, and most of them were - even Tubyaku's speech was sprinkled with Russian, the lingua franca of a forgotten empire - their affirmation of the old cultures was stronger then than ever before. The once dominant discourse of a colonising church and state, of step-mother Russia, had had to yield to the growing assertiveness of the indigenes.

Demography had helped. The one-industry cities set up in Soviet times - Vorkuta, Norilsk, Dikson and a dozen others - had slowly emptied, unable to provide for their ageing inhabitants or attract younger ones. With no road or rail links connecting them to the rest of the country, waterways were their only lifeline. A summer window of four to five months brought the river barges and coasters; in winter the same river, frozen two metres thick, became makeshift highways for tractor trains. Prohibitively expensive, this subsistence support was one of the first victims of retrenchment, despite the rapidly warming climate.

By the end of the second decade of the $21^{st}$ century most of the ten million Russians who had lived above the Arctic Circle had taken the resettlement grants and gone back south, leaving the tundra and taiga to their first inhabitants.

The captain himself was a Nyenets, like them a long uprooted part of the forest, of a pre-technical world, though he would have scorned that last adjective. We saw his framed diplomas on the walls of his cabin. For he, like many others, had risen above the dependent alcoholism of his ancestors, dead in their fifties, aimless, alienated, despised, and increasingly ignorant of their own fragilised culture. Already before the end of the millennium's first century, their forebears had started to repossess it, revive and adapt it, and even started to inspire the populations which had once ignored them as irrelevant.

And so, when the order came to decommission the old ship, the crew had asked for a vessel-cleaning to send it safely to rest. It had been a good ship - they had located hectares of nodule fields on the ocean bed, five methane reservoirs, and two natural gas deposits, the stuff of bonuses. There had been no loss of life, no major accidents, and no inter-ethnic violence. A cousin whose son was on board had contacted Tubyaku, told him what was needed, and the shaman had agreed to come.

*

That was when it was still T8. An initial attempt to divert had failed. So little was needed to make it happen - a reduction in speed of fractions of a second, a deviation of fractions of a degree, would be enough to produce a near miss or even better. But delivering a nuclear payload so far out and sufficiently accurately was a problem. A nuclear explosion two kilometres from the rock would do no more than volatalize a thin layer of the surface. Yet the thrust of the hot gases thus produced would be enough to nudge the impactor onto a different trajectory. In the event it didn't work. The explosion was premature, too far off, and Hofmeister remained on course.

There was increasing pressure to adopt another solution: psychologically satisfying, technically more feasible, right in your face: blow it up, fragment it, with a direct hit from a thermonuclear warhead. But there was a complication - Hofmeister was a contact binary, two giant mountains locked together. And orbiting around them, a miniature moon, half a kilometre wide. The experts knew they could hit it; they also knew that the impactor would cause even greater damage fragmented than whole.

In the event they did not have to make the choice. When the sun flares erupted, that was it. They could see the thing, low in the sky, night and day. It was spectacular, awe-inspiring, fascinating, and yet it was difficult to believe that this was the end, the Ultimate Impact. Torino 10 left no hope, no hiding place. T10 was global. Yet...someone's end, yes, but everybody's, all eleven billion? Some panicked, lighting out for high ground, caves, cathedrals, mosques, synagogues, temples, the ends of the Earth, others jacked in their lives of quiet desperation and began at last to suck out the marrow that had always eluded them, others just crossed their fingers and stayed put, helped in their wishful thinking by the collapse of the global information network. No one had the full story anymore; immediacy had gone. Local stations were still on the air, just, but recycling increasingly old news. Only the grungy prophets of doom with their mad eyes and whiffy pants who daily paraded their message along the shining glass canyons of the world's central business districts had a smile on their faces. *The end of the world is nigh* was no longer the pathetic expression of the touched and disturbed.

\*

As they approached the decommissioning cut, standing with the other off-duty crew on the deck below the sail, Tubyaku and Neiming were as much aware of the asteroid as anyone. There it was, bigger than the moon, almost turning the daytime winter dark to light again. But their thoughts, they told us, were on home, on making it back to the village. They stayed on deck with the others as the lodka made its way up the narrow trench. An occasional shudder ran through the ship as its hull crushed car-sized growlers into the channel wall. Out to sea, larger fragments drifted listlessly, the last reminders of the frozen ocean which had once capped the world.

Beyond the end of the trench lay perhaps twenty or thirty other boats, each in its own sealed sarcophagus. The technique was simple. While construction crews built a coffer dam at the stern of the vessel, wrecking crews cut the sail off flush with the deck. Anything usable or removable was hoisted out through the gaping hole. Then the aperture was plugged with tonnes of concrete and the water pumped out of the dock. The boat settled on the bottom, its deck some fifteen metres below ground level, its reactors much lower. There, uncrushable, sealed by the protective lead-lined shuttering installed around the hull, their radiation and heat could ebb away for centuries, undetectable through the massive concrete overburden which had been poured in above them.

Telling this, Tubyaku had placed his outstretched hands palm downwards before us and moved them back and forth, like detectors, as though waiting to register whatever could get through from below.

Excavated early in the previous century, before the permafrost had relinquished its grip, the trench, like the other four, hundreds of kilometres to the west, had had to be artificially reinforced as the climate warmed.

Winters had still come, but they were shorter, and increasingly less cold. Ground no longer covered by snow absorbed the warmth of the sun again, which melted more snow, pushing the snow cover ever more northwards. Carbon dioxide and methane, trapped in the frozen subsoil for thousands of years, rose into the sky in gigatonne quantities. Temperatures rose 12°, from a summer average of 15° in 2050, when the ice was still breaking up.

With the thaws came not only a deeper carpeting of spring flowers and giant swarms of gnats and black-fly, but the stench of fauna thirteen thousand years dead. The scattered carcasses of mammoths, sabre-toothed cats, mega-elks, giant wolves, mastodons, burped their decomp gases through the thawed ground or lay rotting in the light, exposed by land-slips and subsidence.

(At the village we have a Wonder-Room. Unlike the Settlement one, with its meagre collection of pocketable Earth junk, this one will grow. Who could have smuggled the antlers of a mega-elk on board a hab, or the four molars of a mammoth, as big as stones from an ancient dyke? We have them, and the skull of a dog, we think - the children found it rolling in the surf - but not an ice-age one, just from Tubyaku's time, but no less extinct. They filled the skull with berries, as Neiming told them to. Noho, they've called it.)

As the permafrost retreated deeper and deeper, the timber-line advanced northwards. Increasing warmth dried the water-logged tundra to a less sodden moistness. Ground-hugging plants reached upwards, as though aware that things were changing. Dwarf willows waved their catkins a metre above the ground instead of just above it, and new plants took hold, their seeds blown in by winds from the south. Like humans freed of gravity, birch, alder, larch and spruce grew taller. On the coast, the sea crept up over the land, turning the peninsula to the north-west of what was to become our home into an island and the distant swamps to our west into an inland sea, a thousand kilometres across.

*

Then the impactor hit. Billions drowned in the mile-high tsunamis; billions more were incinerated by the blast. Those who survived the initial destruction died later of cold and starvation. The last few patches of rain forests burned liked tinder; lakes evaporated in the heat; toxic smog rolled across the continents, and acid rain more acid than anything Earth had experienced since Chicxulub had wiped out the dinosaurs scoured the land with its corrosive downpour. No sunlight penetrated the dust cover shrouding the planet.Winter came back with a vengeance. Once unfrozen waterways froze again, but the seas, charged with heat, remained liquid.

Then, slowly, after two years of cold, the darkness yielded to gloom, like the half-dark of a polar night. Later, slivers of sunlight sliced down through rents in the clouds, warming the fungi beneath the soil and the hibernating rodents still just alive in their burrows. Sunlight penetrated the surface ice of frozen bogs and pools, warming the water beneath. Convection currents stirred the liquid. Caught up in the turbulence, nutrients revived the overwintering fish, the larvae, the microscopic algae, the tardigrades, the phytoplankton, worms, rotifers…Photosynthesis started again - aquatic mosses added oxygen to the water. Plants poked through the soil. Primary production, without which nothing can begin - *All flesh is truly "grass"* Paul Ehrlich had said - began again. The bounce-back had started.

The dust cleared, it started to get warm again, and even warmer than before, as greenhouse gases, nature's not man's, spewed out by "long dead" volcanos in the aftermath of Hofmeister trapped the new heat, melting what was left of battered icecaps, temporarily reprieved from disappearance by the post-impact cold. Waterways unfroze, for good.

*

It happened just before they docked. Neiming was going down below, but lost her footing two rungs from the bottom of the ladder, catching her ankle in the process. They heard a scream and found her almost fainting with the pain of it. Unable to walk a step, she allowed herself to be carried aft to the sick bay where the medics gave her a shot and strapped her up. They stayed on board that night, along with the skeleton crew for the decomm. The rest of the crew took the two small cutters back down the trench and into the river to the shore. There the company's hovercraft picked them up and took them back to the base down the coast to the west.

The next day Neiming could barely move, unable even to hobble on her good leg. They might have lifted her into a boat, and would have done sooner had they realised how bad the fracture was, but by the end of the second day it was obvious the boats were not coming back. The radio reports were telling people to stay where they were; phone calls from relatives told them the opposite. Three of the five medics decided to leave, and two of the five-man decomm crew. Boat or no boat, they were not going to stay, and set off in the illuminated dark of those last winter months to follow the river to the coast. They had phones with them and food, just a backpack full each, as though warned of heavy weather ahead, but not much more.

So then there were seven on board. Garrilak, the most senior crewman, was keen to go to but aware that leaving the ship with two strangers on board was not something you were supposed to do. But as another day passed and still no boat had come back he felt himself being torn in two by conflicting senses of duty - stay with the sub, or get back to his young family. The others were in the same position and had told him so.

*I can't leave them by themselves,* he told them, still reasoning as though Torino 10 was just a possibility, not a certainty. The logic of before was reluctant to yield to the overwhelming logic of what was to come.

Day three saw him showing Tubyaku where the food stores were and how to keep the lights and heating and oxygen on.

*It's on low simmer*, he told him, using as homely an image he could think of to explain the state of Reactor 1. Reactor 2 he had shut down completely. He still felt slightly sweaty and loose-bowelled when he thought about what he was doing. But in the absence of calls from headquarters - everyone must have gone already - his feelings of guilt lifted a little as he continued showing Tubyaku the ropes.

He made sure Tub knew about the hatch - how to open it, how to take an air sample without opening it - how to seal off a compartment if there was a breach, how to eject the waste, how to use the periscope, the radio, the microwave oven in the galley, even the big opener for those cans of soup, and how to fire off a flare. He was not so sure that Tubyaku, respected shaman though he was, was up to all this, but at least he was literate, he said to himself, and could just about read the manuals. And the boat wasn't going anywhere. As long as the power lasted they would be okay. Three years was the normal refuelling cycle and here they were at the end of one, but as the damped-down chain reaction only had to keep the lights burning, make air, and power some light equipment, they would get another two years out of it at least. Not that he thought about it that way. He imagined a few weeks maybe, at the outside, then, when things had blown over, people would come and get them out. It would be tricky explaining his actions, but the company would understand. After all, they had abandoned their desks and he was going to abandon his ship.

The farewells were, if not perfunctory, business-like. Neiming was adamant they go and they needed little persuasion. Tubyaku watched them until they were out of site behind a clump of trees. Beneath his feet the deck barely moved in the still water of the cut. Fore and aft, port and starboard, the ropes holding the boat to the bollards softly creaked. He could smell the old truck tires lining the dock side. He went below. As the hatch was closing he heard a bird calling - a brief premonitory shriek. On her cot Neiming was reading.

*

*Eskatalul Neiminga benitek?*
*What did you say to Neiming?* the children asked.

We were sitting around the chart screen, barely visible to one another in the flashlight beam pointing up at the ceiling.

*I told her Lambeyek had spoken: it is coming.*

They knew about Lambeyek - the Eagle god. Even in the humid warmth of that enclosed space I could feel the goosebumps on my arms and from their exchange of glances knew they were feeling the same.

It struck me then that we had more in common than I'd thought. There was no weightlessness, but the same absence of forward momentum, the same waiting, the same silence, the same lone eyeball to the outside…But at least we had known how long it would take. Perhaps it was just as well that they had not.

They had had a week before impact, less than had been reckoned. Inside they felt safe and although Neiming's ankle was improving, they could not have walked far. Better to stay put, in the warmth and light. They had plenty of food, water and oxygen, books, encyclopedias, guides, both e- and paper, and a thousand or more holodiscs of movies, documentaries, language courses, training programmes, cookery classes, self-access programmes in everything from petroglyph cultures of Siberia to the bio-medical applications of nanotechnology, and even Needham's Science and Civilization in China in Russian translation. Tubyaku had devoured the chapter on the compass, his Russian an obstacle at first but increasingly fluent as the months went by.

He showed us how, their first night alone, he had suspended his crozier horizontally under the hatch. It was the same one he had with him then, a thick, man-high stave carved at the top with a face, long and solemn like an Easter Island statue. Beneath, in a lighter wood, was a multi-petalled sun symbol. At the foot of the ladder, he had placed his drum. Then he had brought Neiming to the hatch area, carrying her on his back, and set her down on the blankets and pillows he had already taken from the sick bay. He had put on his face fringe, cut the lights, and there, lulled into a trance by the *houk houk houk* of Neiming's rhythmic shouts and the unyielding dark of the lodka, he slipped into the eternal space behind his eyes and cried out to the helpers to protect him and his family from what was to come.

*

We spent two days at the lodka. The four of us, Kim, Szeto, Mafala and myself, slept outside; we'd had more than our share of living in confined spaces. But Tubyaku and the children slept below. Lijian and Isa were thrilled, and not because this was part of the experience we'd been through on our way here. They'd spent nights in the hab but apart from the constant noise of surf and the awkward slope to the floor, it had been stripped bare over the years. It just wasn't much fun to be in. There, in the lodka, which was far bigger, there was no end of things to explore. Tubyaku knew what everything was and quietly showed off his knowledge of the technology. He might have been a shaman but in the two years on board he had read and watched widely, and knew more than he sometimes let on. We'd suspected that for some time.

And he was honest enough to recognise what he owed that technology; his life for a start, and Neiming's. Without nuclear power, they would have died. Some technology he hated, helicopters for instance. They'd been used for herding reindeer in the time before and made him feel de-skilled and useless. But the detector was something else. You just switched it on; no need to spend a couple of hours invoking its help hoping that the helper would come up with something.

In one of the technical areas, Isa had found the other detector. We learnt long ago that there was no religious significance to all that meticulous criss-crossing of the waters we'd witnessed. A long time before we came it was its twin that Tubyaku had used to try to locate his chest, lost with all their other few possessions when the new lake formed and flooded their encampment. They had strung it between the branches of the raft, half immersed in the water, flush with the reed-covered deck. As the screen on top was difficult to see, you needed to shield out the light with your hands.

They'd done it very scientifically, marking the traverses with upright branches to make sure they covered every square metre of the lake. Of the *chum* and sleds there was no sign but they had hoped that a copper chest would soon reveal itself, lodged at an angle in the thick sediment of the bottom. Just a small box embossed with polar bears and eagles, it fitted neatly across the back of a sled. In it was all his shaman's paraphernalia, the jug for the alcohol poured into the animal's ear, some small figurines, a couple of mirrors, a bottle of vodka, bits of bark and bone, and three very old photographs taken by an Estonian ethnologist of his great great grandfather, Embituk, the shaman of shamans who had disappeared without trace from an Arctic prison in the middle of the 20th century, leaving only an eagle feather behind him. The box remained unfound.

By the time we came across them, they'd long since switched to a different search - for crayfish, great colonies of them. Whenever they used the detector, it was for nothing less practical than that: one day mapping, one day catching. We'd arrived on a mapping day.

Fortunately, there were not so many of us and the crayfish could still replace themselves. But we wondered what would happen if we ever found others who needed them. How long would they last then? What might other communities have that we needed? There has been no sign of other survivors but we live in hope, still do, that one day somewhere round that huge rim of land ringing the top of the world, we might find some.

*

Setting off back home we knew this would be the first of many trips, and not just for the soup cans. We climbed the hill again, pushing off on one foot, the body lifting directly, then the other foot, another lift, so simple, so natural. I thought of our very first days here when it was not so, when every step up a slope left you feeling that you were pushing a plug of earth back into the ground, or walking on a giant treadmill which revolved beneath your feet as you stood still, unmoving.

As we reached the top, the wind whipped at our clothing, streamed the children's long hair behind them, and brought the smell of the sea. White horses raced across the jade-green, choppy waters, darker here and there under the shadow of a few scudding clouds. Straight ahead of us, north, over the top of the world, lay Nunavut, four thousand kilometres away across open water. There was nothing to stop us. No frozen cap, no flesh-eating cold, no narrow, perilous passage of seasonally clear water nipped between land and ice along the coast, north-east along the Asian shore, north-west along the North American. To the west, further still, lay Iceland, and south from there, the Atlantic; to the east, Alaska, and then the Pacific.

There was nowhere we couldn't go. This was *mare nostrum*, our sea, a new Mediterranean, but five times bigger. To the horizon, nothing. Empty. God knows we looked often enough. But not in despair. Around those twenty thousand kilometres of enclosing coast lay the future: new settlements, trade - cabotage at first, from bay to bay, from one peninsula to the next, ports just dozens of kilometres apart - then deep-water voyages, guided only by the sun and stars, to the untapped minerals of Greenland's triple islands, to the green slopes of Spitzbergen, to Novaya Zemlya, Ellesmere Island, Franz-Josef Land, Banks Island, the Novosibirskiye Islands, Severnaya Zemlya, and then from the rim, down, on foot at first, down through the endlessly stretching continents, past the equator, and one day, far, far in the future, past their southern tips, to Antarctica, a world reversed, lying beyond the ocean which encircles it as securely as the land encircles our sea, the last untouched, never ever touched, continent, a vast land of lakes and mountains…and a volcano that only we have seen.

How would it be?

*Li-kerek!* I heard Tubyaku call me. He always called me that - Lijian's father, never Han. Zhudi the same, *Li-nebya*. It was their custom, a sign of respect for parenthood. He beckoned me over. He was pointing into his back-pack, a new one he'd relocated on board. Inside, a thick, oblong shape wrapped in clear plastic. He lifted it out and gave it to me…paper! Hundreds of sheets, smooth, white, razor-edged, bare, waiting to be filled. He'd seen me writing, seen me wrestle with the home-made stuff we'd eventually managed to produce a couple of years before from reeds and twigs, a coarse, unsatisfactory material which snagged and tore and went mouldy in the humidity.

It's still very precious. It has been used sparingly over the six years we have had it, and will be, until we can improve our own. I have had some for writing the rest of my chronicle since then and transcribing what I had already written on the old stuff. The school has had some - a special treat at Life-Giving, a few sheets every year - and Gomez and Szeto, who are keeping a daily record of our lives here.

*

Very late on the last full day back we stopped after crossing the river and made camp by one of the many streams which flowed into it. The brightness had already gone out of sky, and the sun, a dark orange disk, was slowly sinking out of sight below the horizon. It was very quiet. The blustery wind of the previous two days had died out early that morning. An almost imperceptible breeze rustled the bushes around us, frogs croaked hollowly among the rocks, and down below we could hear the sea gently lapping against the beach. Far off to our east, lightning flashed but so far away we heard no sound. Our fire glowed, crackling occasionally, its smoke drifting up into the freshening air.

From low above Taymyr island, a moving glint of silver rose through the gloaming to the zenith. We watched as it passed above us, brightening in the darker sky to the south-east before disappearing from view. We'd seen it before, and some others. The past was still up there, a constant reminder of the future. How long would it be before we could do that again?

The stream burbled past us, down the rocks and into a dark pool. From there a small waterfall plunged into the river, sending out a fan of ripples which the river's slow current pushed impassively out of shape. We were feeling pretty full; we'd opened one of the soup cans (we'd had some in the lodka, T. abstaining) and had talked excitedly about the welcome our find was going to get back at the village. But conversation had dropped off and all of us, even the children, were experiencing the simple pleasure of being at one with the world. I pulled on a stalk of grass and nibbled its whitey green stem, cool and moist and sweet.

*Tsaile, Chinle*
*Water flowing in, flowing out*
*Slow water caught in a pool,*

*Caught in a gourd;*
*Water upon lips, in the throat,*
*Falling upon long hair*
*Loosened in ceremony;*
*Fringes of rain sweeping darkly*
*From the dark side of a cloud,*
*Riding the air in sunlight,*
*Issuing cold from a rock,*
*Transparent as air, or darkened*
*With earth, bloodstained,*
*Grief-heavy;*
*(...)*
*The earth and the sky were constant,*
*But water,*
*How could they name it with one name?*

From Tubyaku the children had learnt all the many terms for snow and ice in Khatavam - the different words for different states - the crusty ice above snow, the sticky, clinging snow of a fresh fall, the compacted hard mass of old snow, the bouncy, thin ice of fresh frozen sea-water, the gravely, dry snow of wind-blown drifts, *imilek* or slush ice, *neged* or anchor ice, and the nightmarish *avik*, the thick slabs of sea ice a hundred metres long which surged onto the land in the unbroken dark of winter, crushing everything before them.

Water was my snow and ice. Rain, drizzle, sea-water, lake water, brackish water, stagnant water, river water, stream water, water in a pool, dew, condensation, fog, moisture, steam, mist, clouds, water in the air - I could tell how humid it was just by sniffing it. I still called it water but I knew what Lewis meant, what the Navajo meant. On Mars, water was $H_2O$, a rare chemical substance. Outside the Settlement there was none, or not enough to mean anything - just a few short-lived puddles, and then rarely. Long ago I had read Guan Zhong and wondered whether ever, ever I would find myself in that lush green world of my dreams whose secret he had proclaimed two and a half thousand years ago.

*People ask what water is. It is the origin of all things, and the ancestral temple of life. It is collected in the heavens and on earth, and stored up in all things. Through it, there is nothing which cannot achieve its germination. It is thus mysterious and magical.*

And then Tubyaku began to sing, not a performance for our benefit, but his own response to the peace of that evening. Lijian joined in. What was it about their singing that seemed to connect me, re-connect me, and all of us, with the irrepressible *qi* of life on Earth? It was visceral, primeval, tactile like a pulse, a beating heart, the music of the unstoppable life-force of Gaia herself.

We got up to fetch wood for the fire and cut some rushes to sleep on. Lijian came over to me. I gave him a goodnight hug, ruffled his hair. Already he was almost as tall as me. Now I look up to him. I was anxious to get home, to Zhudi and Pui and the baby. Ten days away was a long time. We stood quietly together, my arm around his shoulder, looking south.

Among the unchanging stars, a small red spot of light glimmered against the blackness. *Look!* I said, but it had already disappeared behind a bank of cloud.

\*\*\*\*\*

173

# **Postscript**

I have written nothing for two years, at least nothing new, just copied out again my chronicle, one for us, one for posterity - for you, hence the delay. The pace of our life seems to be quickening with every passing month. So many projects now - we have a distinct sense of permanence; we are no longer dried leaves the wind can blow away, but rooted in the landscape, of it, feeling a sense of belonging, of being rightfully here, a feeling of being at the start of something rather than at the end. Seven more children have been born.

We are building a road - the word is inappropriate - but that's what we call it, widening and flattening the track which is already there and putting up shelters along the way. It goes to the lodka - our vast storehouse of gadgets and material and knowledge (*and soup*) adds Pui, my daughter, giggling over my shoulder as I write. We have plundered it frequently, and will go on plundering for years to come.

A pontoon bridge is already in place across the river. When timbers are bigger and there are more of us, we will build a proper one. Next to the lodka we have put up two generators. Pui has rigged up the wiring to its lights - no one taught her this; she just found her own way - and, miracle of miracles, after months poring over the technical manuals, we have got the plasma screens working again, the ones in the crew's quarters and the six big ones on the bridge. They spew out more facts than we can handle, tantalising us with their glowing images of what is possible once we have the manpower and the infrastructure.

Slowly, the future is coming back. We now have access to knowledge again, to know-how, to technology, to maps and charts and survey data, to instructions for building things, making things, finding things. *My new box* Tubyaku calls the lodka, jokingly, but as aware as we are that how we use its treasures is up to us. The hab's screens are still down - have been ever since we got here - and the sea air has not helped. But the hab is the past, a sci-tech relic of another world. Around the lodka a new village is springing up, dominated by the whirling blades of the generators. Thank God for electricity, *dian,* the water of the future. What would we do without it? New huts are going up, a school house as well. Down at the shore the hull of a boat is taking shape, just a small one, but we already know how to sail it from a manual we found in a locker. We still have the hab's parachutes and will cut them up for sails, so it is still good for something, after all.

Tomorrow we have organised a little ceremony: the scaled package, my chronicle, goes into the cavity, a couple of years late, as I said. With it goes a sketch of Tubyaku's halter, a miniature replica of his drum and crozier, a print-out of a map showing what was once magnetic North, a list of our names, with a drop of dried blood against each, and a small packet of rust-coloured dust we bought with us twenty years ago.

And there, just an arm's length from the painting our ancestors made so many millennia ago, our own attempt to communicate across the gulf of time will lie, unseen, until your bright circle of light, flitting

*Duncan Hunter*

dutifully around a cave at first sight as unremarkable as the others you will have explored, suddenly locks on to four inward-pointing arrowheads arranged in a circle - and rock, untouched for aeons, once again feels the warmth of a human hand.

Han

The End

# About the Author

Duncan Hunter, who was born in England in 1943, lives in Hong Kong where he teaches in higher education. In *A Martian Poet in Siberia* he marries a life-long interest in science, and especially in the Planet Mars, to a later interest in poetry, Gaia Theory, Chinese philosophy, and to the complex issues of identity and culture to which his training as a translator and his own culturally-mixed family have made him particularly sensitive.

Printed in the United Kingdom
by Lightning Source UK Ltd.
9689100001B/30-31